50
GREATEST
FOLKTALES

50
GREATEST
FOLKTALES

Published by
Rupa Publications India Pvt. Ltd 2024
7/16, Ansari Road, Daryaganj
New Delhi 110002

Sales centres:
Bengaluru Chennai
Hyderabad Jaipur Kathmandu
Kolkata Mumbai Prayagraj

Edition copyright © Rupa Publications India Pvt. Ltd 2024

All rights reserved.
No part of this publication may be reproduced, transmitted,
or stored in a retrieval system, in any form or by any means,
electronic, mechanical, photocopying, recording or otherwise,
without the prior permission of the publisher.

P-ISBN: 978-93-6156-902-9
E-ISBN: 978-93-6156-073-6

First impression 2024

10 9 8 7 6 5 4 3 2 1

Printed in India

This book is sold subject to the condition that it shall not,
by way of trade or otherwise, be lent, resold, hired out, or otherwise
circulated, without the publisher's prior consent, in any form of
binding or cover other than that in which it is published.

Contents

1. What Makes the Eclipse — 1
    (Indian, Khasi)
2. The Soul That Lived in the Bodies of All Beasts — 7
    (Greenland, Eskimo)
3. A Story of the Fox — 12
    (Korean)
4. The Lark and the Toad — 14
    (French)
5. The Seven Brothers Simeon — 19
    (Russian)
6. The Ungrateful Man — 26
    (West African)
7. The Magic Mirror — 29
    (Spanish)
8. The Prince Who Befriended the Beasts — 34
    (Mingrelian)
9. Father Frost — 39
    (Russian)
10. The Goddess Who Came to Live with Mankind — 43
    (Indian, Khasi)
11. The Wolf-Child — 49
    (Spanish/Portuguese)

12. How Wisdom Became the Property of
    the Human Race   55
    (West African)

13. The Man with His Leg Tied Up   57
    (Native American)

14. Crocodile's Treason   64
    (South African)

15. Two Brothers   70
    (Georgian)

16. Wirreenun the Rainmaker   74
    (Australian)

17. The Story of Sayen   79
    (Filipino)

18. How the Tiger Got His Stripes   83
    (Brazilian)

19. The King and the Apple   89
    (Georgian)

20. The Fairy Bonze   93
    (Chinese)

21. The Strong Man and the Dwarf   107
    (Gurian)

22. The Enchanted Princesses   111
    (Czech)

23. Danílo the Unfortunate   120
    (Russian)

24. The Twin Brothers   128
    (Czech)

25. The Fox and the King's Son (Georgian)	135
26. The Mistaken Gifts (Filipino)	142
27. The Eagle and the Whale (Greenland, Eskimo)	144
28. The Vengeance of the Goddess (Chinese)	148
29. The Two Cats (Arabic)	160
30. The Indigent Brahman (Indian)	165
31. How We Got the Name 'Spider Tales' (West African)	174
32. Dogedog (Filipino)	176
33. Aponibolinayen (Filipino)	180
34. The Plucky Maiden (Korean)	186
35. Lumabet (Filipino, Bagobo)	191
36. The Goblins Turned to Stone (Dutch)	194
37. The White Trout (Irish)	200
38. The Ghost-Brahman (Indian)	204

39. The Haughty Princess (Irish)	208
40. The Widow's Son (Subanun)	212
41. How Mushrooms First Grew (West African)	217
42. The Demon Cat (Irish)	220
43. The Woman Who Had a Bear as a Foster-Son (Greenland, Eskimo)	223
44. The First Month (Japanese)	228
45. The Man Who Met Misery (Czech)	237
46. The Origin of the Narran Lake (Australian)	240
47. The Little House (French)	244
48. The Legend of the Wooden Shoe (Dutch)	249
49. Why Dogs Wag Their Tails (Visayan)	257
50. The Watchful Servant (Spanish)	259

1

What Makes the Eclipse

(Indian, Khasi)

Very early in the history of the world a beautiful female child, whom the parents called Ka Nam, was born to a humble family who lived in a village on the borders of one of the great Khasi forests. She was such a beautiful child that her mother constantly expressed her fears lest some stranger passing that way might kidnap her or cast an 'evil eye' upon her, so she desired to bring her up in as much seclusion as their poor circumstances would permit. To this the father would not agree; he told his wife not to harbour foolish notions, but to bring up the child naturally like other people's children, and teach her to work and to make herself useful. So Ka Nam was brought up like other children, and taught to work and to make herself useful.

One day, as she was taking her pitcher to the well, a big tiger came out of the forest and carried her to his lair. She was terrified almost to death, for she knew that the tigers were the most cruel of all beasts. The name of this tiger was U Khla, and his purpose in carrying off the maiden was to eat her, but when he saw how young and small she was, and that she would not suffice for one full meal for him, he decided to keep her in his lair until she grew bigger.

He took great care of her and brought home to her many delicacies which her parents had never been able to afford, and as she never suspected the cruel designs of the tiger, she soon grew to feel quite at home and contented in the wild beast's den, and she grew up to be a maiden of unparalleled loveliness.

The tiger was only waiting his opportunity, and when he saw that she had grown up he determined to kill her, for he was longing to eat the beautiful damsel whom he had fed with such care. One day, as he busied himself about his lair, he began to mutter to himself: 'Now the time has come when I can repay myself for all my trouble in feeding this human child; to-morrow I will invite all my fellow-tigers here and we will feast upon the maiden.'

It happened that a little mouse was foraging near the den at that time and she overheard the tiger muttering to himself. She was very sorry for the maiden, for she knew that she was alone and friendless and entirely at the mercy of the tiger; so the little mouse went and told the maiden that the tigers were going to kill her and eat her on the following day. Ka Nam was in great distress and wept very bitterly. She begged of the mouse to help her to escape, and the mouse, having a tender heart, gave her what aid was in her power.

In the first place she told the maiden to go out of the den and to seek the cave of the magician, U Hynroh, the Giant Toad, to whom the realm was under tribute. He was a peevish and exacting monster from whom every one recoiled, and Ka Nam would have been terrified to approach him under ordinary conditions, but the peril which faced her gave her courage, and under the guidance of the mouse she went to the toad's cave. When he saw her and beheld how fair she was, and learned how she had been the captive of his old rival the tiger, he readily consented to give her his protection; so he clothed her in a toadskin, warning her not to divest herself of it in the presence of others on pain of death. This he did in order to keep the maiden in his own custody and to make her his slave.

When the mouse saw that her beautiful friend had been transformed into the likeness of a hideous toad she was very sorrowful, and regretted having sent her to seek the protection of U Hynroh, for she knew that as long as she remained in the jungle Ka Nam would be henceforth forced to live with the toads and to be their slave. So she led her away secretly and brought her to the magic tree which was in that jungle, and told the maiden to climb into the tree that she might be transported to the sky, where she would be safe from harm for ever. So the maid climbed into the magic tree and spoke the magic words taught her by the mouse: 'Grow tall, dear tree, the sky is near, expand and grow.' Upon which the tree began to expand upwards till its branches touched the sky, and then the maiden alighted in the Blue Realm and the tree immediately dwindled to its former size.

By and by the tiger and his friends arrived at the den, ravenous for their feast, and when he found that his prey had disappeared his disappointment and anger knew no bounds and were terrible to witness. He uttered loud threats for vengeance on whoever had connived at the escape of his captive, and his roars were so loud that the animals in the jungle trembled with fear. His fellow-tigers also became enraged when they understood that they had been deprived of their feast, and they turned on U Khla and in their fury tore him to death.

Meanwhile Ka Nam wandered homeless in the Blue Realm, clothed in the toadskin. Every one there lived in palaces and splendour, and they refused to admit the loathsome, venomous-looking toad within their portals, while she, mindful of the warning of U Hynroh, the magician, feared to uncover herself. At last she appeared before the palace of Ka Sngi, the Sun, who, ever gracious and tender, took pity on her and permitted her to live in a small outhouse near the palace.

One day, thinking herself to be unobserved, the maid put aside her covering of toadskin and sat to rest awhile in her small room, but before going abroad she carefully wrapped herself in the skin as before. She was accidentally seen by the son of Ka Sngi, who was a very noble youth. He was astonished beyond words to find a maiden of such rare beauty hiding herself beneath a hideous toadskin and living in his mother's outhouse, and he marvelled what evil spell had caused her to assume such a loathsome covering. Her beauty enthralled him and he fell deeply in love with her.

He hastened to make his strange discovery known to his mother, and entreated her to lodge the maiden without delay in the palace and to let her become his wife. Ka Sngi, having the experience and foresight of age, determined to wait before acceding to the request of her young and impetuous son until she herself had ascertained whether a maid such as her son described really existed beneath the toadskin, or he had been deluded by some evil enchantment into imagining that he had seen a maiden in the outhouse.

So Ka Sngi set herself to watch the movements of the toad in the outhouse, and one day, to her surprise and satisfaction, she beheld the maiden uncovered, and was astonished at her marvellous beauty and pleasing appearance. But she did not want her son to rush into an alliance with an enchanted maiden, so she gave him a command that he should not go near or speak to the maid until the toadskin had been destroyed and the evil spell upon her broken. Once again Ka Sngi set herself to watch the movements of the toad, and one day her vigilance was rewarded by discovering Ka Nam asleep with the toadskin cast aside. Ka Sngi crept stealthily and seized the toadskin and burned it to ashes. Henceforth the maiden appeared in her own natural form, and lived very happily as the wife of Ka Sngi's son, released for ever from the spell of the Giant Toad.

There was an old feud between U Hynroh and Ka Sngi because she refused to pay him tribute, and when he learned that she had wilfully destroyed the magic skin in which he had wrapped the maiden, his anger was kindled against Ka Sngi, and he climbed up to the Blue Realm to devour her. She bravely withstood him, and a fierce struggle ensued which was witnessed by the whole universe.

When mankind saw the conflict they became silent, subdued with apprehension lest the cruel monster should conquer their benefactress. They uttered loud cries and began to beat mournfully on their drums till the world was full of sound and clamour.

Like all bullies, U Hynroh was a real coward at heart, and when he heard the noise of drums and shouting on the earth, his heart melted within him with fear, for he thought it was the tramp of an advancing army coming to give him battle. He quickly released his hold upon Ka Sngi and retreated with all speed from the Blue Realm. Thus mankind were the unconscious deliverers of their noble benefactress from the hand of her cruel oppressor.

U Hynroh continues to make periodical attacks on the sun to this day, and in many countries people call the attacks 'Eclipses', but the Ancient Khasis, who saw the great conflict, knew it to be the Giant Toad, the great cannibal, trying to devour Ka Sngi. He endeavours to launch his attacks when the death of some great personage in the world is impending, hoping to catch mankind too preoccupied to come to the rescue. Throughout the whole of Khasi-land to this day it is the custom to beat drums and to raise a loud din whenever there is an eclipse.

2

The Soul That Lived in the Bodies of All Beasts

(Greenland, Eskimo)

There was a man whose name was Avôvang. And of him it is said that nothing could wound him. And he lived at Kangerdlugssuaq.

At that time of the year when it is good to be out, and the days do not close with dark night, and all is nearing the great summer, Avôvang's brother stood one day on the ice near the breathing hole of a seal.

And as he stood there, a sledge came dashing up, and as it reached him, the man who was in it said:

'There will come many sledges to kill your brother.'

The brother now ran into the house to tell what he had heard. And then he ran up a steep rocky slope and hid away.

The sledges drove up before the house, and Avôvang went out to meet them, but he took with him the skin of a dog's neck, which had been used to wrap him in when he was a child. And when then the men fell upon him, he simply placed that piece of skin on the ground and stood on it, and all his enemies could not wound him with their weapons, though they stabbed again and again.

At last he spoke, and said mockingly:

'All my body is now like a piece of knotty wood, with the scars of the wounds you gave me, and yet you could not bring about my death.'

And as they could not wound him with their stabbing, they dragged him up to the top of a high cliff, thinking to cast him down. But each time they caught hold of him to cast him down, he changed himself into another man who was not their enemy. And at last they were forced to drive away, without having done what they wished.

It is also told of Avôvang, that he once desired to travel to the south, and to the people who lived in the south, to buy wood. This men were wont to do in the old days, but now it is no longer so.

And so they set off, many sledges together, going southward to buy wood. And having done what they wished, they set out for home. On the way, they had made a halt to look for the breathing holes of seal, and while the men had been thus employed, the women had gone on. Avôvang had taken a wife on that journey, from among the people of the south.

And while the men stood there looking for seal holes, all of them felt a great desire to possess Avôvang's wife, and therefore they tried to kill him. Qautaq stabbed him in the eyes, and the others caught hold of him and sent him sliding down through a breathing hole into the sea.

When his wife saw this, she was angry, and taking the wood which they had brought from the south, she broke it all into small pieces. So angry was she at thus being made a widow.

Then she went home, after having spoiled the men's wood. But the sledges drove on.

Suddenly a great seal came up ahead of them, right in their way, where the ice was thin and slippery. And the sledges drove straight at it, but many fell through and were drowned at that hunting. And a little after, they again saw something in their way. It was a fox, and they set off in chase, but driving at furious speed up a mountain of screw-ice, they were dashed down and killed. Only two men escaped, and they made their way onward and told what had come to the rest.

And it was the soul of Avôvang, whom nothing could wound, that had changed, first into a seal and then into a fox, and thus brought about the death of his enemies. And afterwards he made up his mind to let himself be born in the shape of every beast on earth, that he might one day tell his fellow-men the manner of their life.

At one time he was a dog, and lived on meat which he stole from the houses. When he was pressed for food, he would carefully watch the men about the houses, and eat anything they threw away.

But Avôvang soon tired of being a dog, on account of the many beatings which fell to his lot in that life. And so he made up his mind to become a reindeer.

At first he found it far from easy, for he could not keep pace with the other reindeer when they ran.

'How do you stretch your hind legs at a gallop?' he asked one day.

'Kick out towards the farthest edge of the sky,' they answered. And he did so, and then he was able to keep pace with them.

But at first he did not know what he should eat, and therefore he asked the others.

'Eat moss and lichen,' they said.

And he soon grew fat, with thick suet on his back.

But one day the herd was attacked by a wolf, and all the reindeer dashed out into the sea, and there they met some kayaks in their flight, and one of the men killed Avôvang.

He cut him up, and laid the meat in a cairn of stones. And there he lay, and when the winter came, he longed for the men to come and bring him home. And glad was he one day to hear the stones rattling down, and when they commenced to eat him, and cracked the bones with pieces of rock to get at the marrow, Avôvang escaped and changed himself into a wolf.

And now he lived as a wolf, but here as before he found that he could not keep up with his comrades at a run. And they ate all the food, so that he got none.

'Kick up towards the sky,' they told him. And then at once he was able to overtake all the reindeer, and thus get food.

And later he became a walrus, but found himself unable to dive down to the bottom; all he could do was to swim straight ahead through the water.

'Take off as if from the middle of the sky; that is what we do when we dive to the bottom,' said the others. And so he swung his hindquarters up to the sky, and down he went to the bottom. And his comrades taught him what to eat; mussels and little white stones.

Once also he was a raven. 'The ravens never lack food,' he said, 'but they often feel cold about the feet.'

Thus he lived the life of every beast on earth. And at last he became a seal again. And there he would lie under the ice, watching the men who came to catch him. And being a great wizard, he was able to hide himself away under the nail of a man's big toe.

But one day there came a man out hunting who had cut off the nail of his big toe. And that man harpooned him. Then they hauled him up on the ice and took him home.

Inside the house, they began cutting him up, and when the man cast the mittens to his wife, Avôvang went with them, and crept into the body of the woman. And after a time he was born again, and became once more a man.

卍

3

A Story of the Fox

(Korean)

[The Fox.—Orientals say that among the long-lived creatures are the tortoise, the deer, the crane and the fox, and that these long-lived ones attain to special states of spiritual refinement. If trees exist through long ages they become coal; if pine resin endures it becomes amber; so the fox, if it lives long, while it never becomes an angel, or spiritual being, as a man does, takes on various metamorphoses, and appears on earth in various forms.]

Yi Kwai was the son of a minister. He passed his examinations and held high office. When his father was Governor of Pyong-an Province, Kwai was a little boy and accompanied him. The Governor's first wife being dead, Kwai's stepmother was the mistress of the home. Once when His Excellency had gone out on an inspecting tour, the yamen was left vacant, and Kwai was there with her. In the rear garden of the official quarters was a pavilion, called the Hill Pagoda, that was connected by a narrow gateway with the public hall. Frequently Kwai took one of the yamen boys with him and went there to study, and once at night when it had grown late and the boy who accompanied him had taken his departure, the door opened suddenly and a young woman came in. Her clothes were neat and clean, and she was very pretty. Kwai looked carefully at her, but did not recognize her. She was evidently a stranger, as there was no such person among the dancing-girls of the yamen.

He remained looking at her, in doubt as to who she was, while she on the other hand took her place in the corner of the room and said nothing.

'Who are you?' he asked. She merely laughed and made no reply. He called her. She came and knelt down before him, and he took her by the hand and patted her shoulder, as though he greeted her favourably. The woman smiled and pretended to enjoy it. He concluded, however, that she was not a real woman, but a goblin of some kind, or perhaps a fox, and what to do he knew not. Suddenly he decided on a plan, caught her, swung her on to his back, and rushed out through the gate into the yamen quarters, where he shouted at the top of his voice for his stepmother and the servants to come.

It was midnight and all were asleep. No one replied, and no one came. The woman, then, being on his back, bit him furiously at the nape of the neck. By this he knew that she was the fox. Unable to stand the pain of it, he loosened his grasp, when she jumped to the ground, made her escape and was seen no more.

What a pity that no one came to Kwai's rescue and so made sure of the beast!

4

The Lark and the Toad

(French)

There was once a pretty woman named Agnella, who cultivated a farm. She lived alone with a young servant named Passerose. The farm was small but beautiful and in fine order. She had a most charming cow, which gave a quantity of milk, a cat to destroy the mice and an ass to carry her fruit, butter, vegetables, eggs and cheese to markets every Wednesday.

No one knew up to that time how Agnella and Passerose had arrived at this unknown farm which received in the county the name of the Woodland Farm.

One evening Passerose was busy milking the pretty white cow while Agnella prepared the supper. At the moment she was placing some good soup and a plate of cream upon the table, she saw an enormous toad devouring with avidity some cherries which had been put on the ground in a vine-leaf.

'Ugly toad!' exclaimed Agnella, 'I will teach you how to eat my cherries!' At the same moment she lifted the leaves which contained the cherries, and gave the toad a kick which dashed it off about ten steps. She was about to throw it from the door, when the toad uttered a sharp whistle and raised itself upon its hind legs; its great eyes were flashing, and its enormous mouth opening and shutting with rage, its whole ugly body was trembling and from its quivering throat was heard a terrible bellowing.

Agnella paused in amazement; she recoiled, indeed, to avoid the venom of the monstrous and enraged toad. She looked around for a broom to eject this hideous monster, when the toad advanced towards her, made with its fore paws a gesture of authority, and said in a voice trembling with rage:—

'You have dared to touch me with your foot! You have prevented me from satisfying my appetite with the cherries which you had placed within my reach! You have tried to expel me from your house! My vengeance shall reach you and will fall upon that which you hold most dear! You shall know and feel that the fairy Furious is not to be insulted with impunity. You shall have a son, covered with coarse hair like a bear's cub and—'

'Stop, sister,' interrupted a small voice, sweet and flute-like, which seemed to come from above. Agnella raised her head and saw a lark perched on the top of the front door. 'You revenge yourself too cruelly for an injury inflicted, not upon you in your character of a fairy but upon the ugly and disgusting form in which it has pleased you to disguise yourself. By my power, which is superior to yours, I forbid you to exaggerate the evil which you have already done in your blind rage and which, alas! it is not in my power to undo. And you, poor mother,' she continued, turning to Agnella, 'do not utterly despair; there is a possible remedy for the deformity of your child. I will accord to him the power of changing his skin with any one whom he may, by his goodness and service rendered, inspire with sufficient gratitude and affection to consent to the change. He will then resume the handsome form which would have been his if my sister, the fairy Furious, had not given you this terrible proof of her malice and cruelty.'

'Alas! Madam Lark,' replied Agnella, 'all this goodness cannot prevent my poor, unhappy son from being disgusting and like a wild beast. His very playmates will shun him as a monster.'

'That is true,' replied the fairy Drolette; 'and the more so as it is forbidden to yourself or to Passerose to change skins with him. But I will neither abandon you nor your son. You will name him Ourson until the day when he can assume a name worthy of his birth and beauty. He must then be called the prince Marvellous.'

Saying these words, the fairy flew lightly through the air and disappeared from sight.

The fairy Furious withdrew, filled with rage, walking slowly and turning every instant to gaze at Agnella with a menacing air. As she moved slowly along, she spat her venom from side to side and the grass, the plants and the bushes perished along her course. This was a venom so subtle that nothing could ever flourish on the spot again and the path is called to this day the Road of the Fairy Furious.

When Agnella found herself alone, she began to sob. Passerose, who had finished her work and saw the hour of supper approaching, entered the dining-room and with great surprise saw her mistress in tears.

'Dear queen, what is the matter? Who can have caused you this great grief? I have seen no one enter the house.'

'No one has entered, my dear, except those who enter everywhere. A wicked fairy under the form of a toad and a good fairy under the appearance of a lark.'

'And what have these fairies said to you, my queen, to

make you weep so piteously? Has not the good fairy interfered to prevent the misfortunes which the wicked fairy wished to bring about?'

'No, my dear friend. She has somewhat lightened them but it was not in her power to set them aside altogether.'

Agnella then recounted all that had taken place and that she would have a son with a skin like a bear. At this narrative Passerose wept as bitterly as her mistress.

'What a misfortune!' she exclaimed. 'What degradation and shame, that the heir of a great kingdom should be a bear! What will King Ferocious, your husband, say if he should ever discover us?'

'And how will he ever find us, Passerose? You know that after our flight we were swept away by a whirlwind and dashed from cloud to cloud for twelve hours with such astonishing rapidity that we found ourselves more than three thousand leagues from the kingdom of Ferocious. Besides, you know his wickedness. You know how bitterly he hates me since I prevented him from killing his brother Indolent and his sister Nonchalante. You know that I fled because he wished to kill me also. I have no reason to fear that he will pursue me for I am sure that he will wish never to see me again.'

Passerose, after having wept and sobbed some time with the Queen Aimee, for that was her true name, now entreated her mistress to be seated at the table.

'If we wept all night, dear queen, we could not prevent your son from being shaggy but we will endeavor to educate him so well, to make him so good, that he will not be a long time in finding some good and grateful soul who will exchange a white skin for this hairy one which the evil fairy Furious has put upon him. A beautiful present indeed! She would have done well to reserve it for herself.'

The poor queen, whom we will continue to call Agnella for fear of giving information to King Ferocious, rose slowly, dried her eyes and succeeded in somewhat overcoming her sadness. Little by little the gay and cheering conversation of Passerose dissipated her forebodings. Before the close of the evening, Passerose had convinced her that Ourson would not remain a long time a bear; that he would soon resume a form worthy of a noble prince. That she would herself indeed be most happy to exchange with him, if the fairy would permit it.

Agnella and Passerose now retired to their chambers and slept peacefully.

5

The Seven Brothers Simeon

(Russian)

There were once upon a time two old serfs, who lived together for many years without children; and in their old age they prayed for a child to keep them from want when they were no longer able to labour. After seven years the good woman gave birth to seven sons, who were all named Simeon; but when these boys were in their tenth year, the old folk died, and the sons tilled the ground which their father left them.

It chanced one day that the Tsar Ador drove past, and wondered sore to see such little fellows all busy at work in their field. So he sent his oldest boyar to ask them whose children they were, and why they were working so hard, and the eldest Simeon answered, that they were orphans, and had no one to work for them, and that they were all called Simeon. When the boyar told this to Tsar Ador, he ordered the boys to be brought along with him.

On returning to the palace, the Tsar called together all his boyars, and asked their advice, saying: 'My boyars, you see here seven poor orphans, who have no kinsfolk; I am resolved to make such men of them that they shall hereafter have cause to thank me; and therefore I ask your advice—what handicraft or art shall I have them taught?' Then the boyars replied: 'Your Majesty, seeing that they are old enough to have understanding, it would be well to ask each brother separately what craft he wishes to learn.'

This answer pleased the Tsar, and he said to the eldest Simeon: 'Tell me, friend, what art or trade would you like to learn? I will apprentice you to it.' But Simeon answered: 'Please your Majesty, I wish to learn no art; but if you will command a smithy to be put up in the middle of your court, I will raise a column which shall reach to the sky.' By this time the Tsar at once saw that the first Simeon wanted indeed no teaching if he was so good a smith as to do such work; but he did not believe that he could make so tall a pillar; so he ordered a smithy to be built in his courtyard, and the eldest Simeon straightway set to work.

Then the Tsar asked the second Simeon: 'What craft or art would you learn, my friend?' and the lad replied: 'Your Majesty, I will learn neither craft nor art; but when my eldest brother has smithied the iron column, I will mount to the top of it, look around over the whole world, and tell you what is passing in every kingdom.' So the Tsar saw there was clearly no need to teach this brother, as he was clever enough already.

Thereupon he questioned the third Simeon: 'What craft or what art will you learn?' He replied: 'Your Majesty, I want to learn neither craft nor art; but if my eldest brother will make me an axe I will build a ship in the twinkling of an eye.' When the Tsar heard this he exclaimed: 'Such master workers are just the men I want! Thou also hast nothing to learn.'

Then he asked the fourth Simeon: 'Thou Simeon, what craft or what art will thou learn?' and he answered: 'Your Majesty,

I need to learn nothing; but when my third brother has built a ship, and the ship is attacked by enemies, I will seize it by the prow, and draw it into the kingdom under the earth; and when the foe has departed, I will bring it back again upon the sea.' The Tsar was astonished at such marvels, and replied: 'In truth you have nothing to learn.'

Then he asked the fifth Simeon: 'What trade or what art would you learn, Simeon?' And he replied: 'I need none, your Majesty; but when my eldest brother has made me a gun, I will shoot with it every bird that flies, however distant, if I can see it.' And the Tsar said: 'You'll be a famous hunter truly!'

The Tsar now asked the sixth Simeon: 'What art will you learn?' and he replied in like manner: 'Sire, I will follow no art, but when my fifth brother has shot a bird in the air I will catch it before it falls to the ground, and bring it to your Majesty.' 'Bravo!' said the Tsar; 'you will serve in the field as well as a retriever.'

Thereupon the Tsar enquired of the last Simeon what craft or art he would learn. 'Your Majesty,' he replied, 'I will learn neither craft nor trade, for I am already skilled in a precious art.' 'What kind of art do you understand then?' said the Tsar. 'I understand how to steal better than any man alive.' When the Tsar heard of such a wicked art, he grew angry, and said to his boyars: 'My Lords, how do you advise me to punish this thief Simeon? What death shall he die?' But they all replied: 'Wherefore, O Tsar, should he die? Who knows but that he may be a clever thief, and prove useful in case of need?' 'How so?' said the Tsar. 'Your Majesty,' replied the boyars, 'has for ten long years sued for the hand of the beautiful Tsarina Helena in vain, and has already lost many armies and great store of money. Who knows but that this thief Simeon may in some way steal the fair Tsarina for your Majesty.'

'Well spoken, my friends,' replied the Tsar; and, turning to the thief Simeon, he said: 'Hark you, friend, can you pass through thrice nine lands into the thirtieth kingdom and steal for me the fair Queen Helena? I am in love with her, and if you can bring her to me I will reward you richly.'

'Leave it to us,' answered Simeon; 'your Majesty has only to command.'

'I do not order you, I entreat you then,' said the Tsar, 'not to tarry longer at my Court, but take with you all the armies and treasure you require.' 'I want not your armies nor your treasure,' said Simeon; 'only send us brothers forth together; without the rest I can do nothing.' The Tsar was unwilling to let them all go; nevertheless he was obliged to consent.

Meanwhile the eldest Simeon had finished the iron column in the smithy of the palace-yard. Then the second Simeon climbed up it, and looked around on all sides, to see whereabouts the kingdom of fair Helena's father lay; and presently he called out to the Tsar Ador: 'Please, your Majesty, beyond thrice nine lands, in the thirtieth kingdom, sits the fair Tsarina at her window. How beautiful she is! One can see the very marrow of her bones, her skin is so clear.' On hearing this the Tsar was more in love than ever, and cried aloud to the Simeons: 'My friends, set out instantly on your journey, and come back as soon as possible; I can no longer live without the fair Tsarina.'

So the eldest Simeon made for the third brother a gun, and took bread for their travels; and the thief Simeon took a cat with him, and so they set out. Now thief Simeon had so accustomed this cat to him, that she ran after him everywhere like a dog; and whenever he stopped, she sat up on her hind legs, rubbed her coat against him and purred. So they all went their way, until they came to the shore of the sea over which they must sail. For a long time they wandered about, seeking wood, to build a ship with. At last they found a huge oak. Then the third Simeon took his axe and laid it at the root of the tree, and in the twinkling of an eye the oak was felled, and a ship built from it, fully rigged, and in the ship there were all kinds of costly wares.

After some months' voyage they arrived safely at the place to which they were bound, and cast anchor. The next day Simeon the thief took his cat and went into the city; and walking straight up to the Tsar's palace, he stood under the window of Queen Helena. Immediately his cat sat up on her hind legs, and fell to rubbing him and purring. But you must know that no cat had ever been seen or heard of in this country, nor was anything known of such an animal.

The fair Tsarina Helena was sitting at her window, and observing the cat, she sent her attendants to inquire of Simeon what kind of animal it was, and whether he would sell it, and for how much. And when the servants asked him, Simeon replied: 'Tell her Majesty that this creature is called a cat, but I cannot consent to sell her; if, however, her Majesty pleases, I shall have the honour of presenting the cat to her.'

So the attendants ran back and told what they had heard from Simeon; and when the Tsarina Helena knew it, she was overjoyed, and went herself to him, and asked why he would not sell it, but would only give it to her. Then she took the cat in her arms, went into her room, and invited Simeon to accompany her; and, going to her father, the Tsar Sarg, the Tsarina showed him the cat, and told him that a stranger had presented it to her. The Tsar gazed at the wonderful animal with delight, and commanded the thief Simeon to be summoned; and when he came, the Tsar wanted to reward him richly for the cat. But Simeon would not take anything; and the Tsar said: 'Stay here in my palace for a time, and meanwhile the cat will become better used to my daughter in your presence.'

Simeon, however, had no desire to remain, and answered: 'Your Majesty, I would stay in your palace with pleasure had I not a ship, in which I came to your kingdom, and which I cannot entrust to anyone; but if your Majesty pleases, I will come every day to the palace and accustom the cat to your fair daughter.'

This offer pleased the Tsar: so every day Simeon went to the fair Queen; and once he said to her: 'Gracious Lady, Your Majesty, often as I have come to visit you, I have not observed that you ever go out to take a walk. If you will come once on board my ship, I will show you a quantity of fine wares, diamonds and gold brocades, more beautiful than you have ever seen before.' Thereupon the Tsarina went to her father and asked his permission to take a walk upon the quay. The Tsar consented, bidding her take her attendants and lady's-maids with her.

When they came to the quay, Simeon invited the Tsarina on board his ship, where he and his brothers displayed to her all kinds of wares. Then said Simeon the thief to the fair Helena: 'You must order your attendants to leave the ship, and I will show you some more costly wares which they must not see.' So the Tsarina ordered them to return to shore; and Simeon the thief instantly desired his brothers to cut the cable, set all the sails, and put out to sea.

Meantime he amused the Tsarina by unpacking the wares and making her various presents. In this manner hours passed by; and at last she told him it was time for her to return home, as her father would be expecting her back. So saying, she went up from the cabin and perceived that the ship was already far out at sea, and almost out of sight of land. Thereat she beat her breast, changed herself into a swan, and flew away. But in an instant the fifth Simeon seizing his gun, fired at her; and the sixth brother caught her before she fell into the water, and placed her on the deck, when the Tsarina changed back into a woman.

Meanwhile the attendants and lady's-maids, who were standing on the shore, and had seen the ship sail away with the Tsarina, went and told the Tsar of Simeon's treachery. Then the Tsar instantly commanded his whole fleet to go in pursuit; and it had already got very near to the Simeons' ship when the fourth brother seized the vessel by the prow and drew it into the subterranean region. When the ship disappeared, all the sailors in the fleet thought it had sunk, together with the beautiful Tsarina Helena, and went back to the Tsar Sarg and told him the sad tidings. But the seven brothers Simeon returned safely to their own country, and conducted the Tsarina Helena to Tsar Ador, who gave the Simeons their freedom as a reward for the services they had rendered, together with much gold and silver and precious stones. And the Tsar lived with the beautiful Queen Helena for many years in peace and happiness.

6

The Ungrateful Man

(West African)

A hunter, who was terribly poor, was one day walking through the forest in search of food. Coming to a deep hole, he found there a leopard, a serpent, a rat, and a man. These had all fallen into the trap and were unable to get out again. Seeing the hunter, they begged him to help them out of the hole.

At first he did not wish to release any but the man. The leopard, he said, had often stolen his cattle and eaten them. The serpent very frequently bit men and caused their death. The rat did no good to any one. He saw no use in setting them free.

However, these animals pleaded so hard for life that at last he helped them out of the pit. Each, in turn, promised to reward him for his kindness—except the man. He, saying he was very poor, was taken home by the kind-hearted hunter and allowed to stay with him.

A short time after, Serpent came to the hunter and gave him a very powerful antidote for snake-poison. 'Keep it carefully,' said Serpent. 'You will find it very useful one day. When you are using it, be sure to ask for the blood of a traitor to mix with it.' The hunter, having thanked Serpent very much, took great care of the powder and always carried it about with him.

The leopard also showed his gratitude by killing animals for the hunter and supplying him with food for many weeks.

Then, one day, the rat came to him and gave him a large bundle. 'These,' said he, 'are some native cloths, gold dust and ivory. They will make you rich.' The hunter thanked the rat very heartily and took the bundle into his cottage.

After this the hunter was able to live in great comfort. He built himself a fine new house and supplied it with everything needful. The man whom he had taken out of the pit still lived with him.

This man, however, was of a very envious disposition. He was not at all pleased at his host's good fortune, and only waited an opportunity to do him some harm. He very soon had a chance.

A proclamation was sounded throughout the country to say that some robbers had broken into the King's palace and stolen his jewels and many other valuables. The ungrateful man instantly hurried to the King and asked what the reward would be if he pointed out the thief. The King promised to give him half of the things which had been stolen. The wicked fellow thereupon falsely accused his host of the theft, although he knew quite well that he was innocent.

The honest hunter was immediately thrown into prison. He was then brought into Court and requested to show how he had become so rich. He told them, faithfully, the source of his income, but no one believed him. He was condemned to die the following day at noon.

Next morning, while preparations were being made for his execution, word was brought to the prison that the King's eldest son had been bitten by a serpent and was dying. Any one who could cure him was begged to come and do so.

The hunter immediately thought of the powder which his serpent friend had given him, and asked to be allowed to use it. At first they were unwilling to let him try, but finally he received permission. The King asked him if there were anything he needed for it and he replied, 'A traitor's blood to mix it with.' His Majesty immediately pointed out the wicked fellow who had accused the hunter and said: 'There stands the worst traitor—for he gave up the kind host who had saved his life.' The man was at once beheaded and the powder was mixed as the serpent had commanded. As soon as it was applied to the prince's wound the young man was cured. In great delight, the King loaded the hunter with honours and sent him happily home.

7

The Magic Mirror

(Spanish)

It was proclaimed throughout the kingdom of Granada that the king had decided on marrying. The news was first told to the court barber, then to the night watchmen, and, in the third place, to the oldest woman in the city of Granada.

The barber told all his customers, who again told all their friends. The night watchmen in crying the hour proclaimed the news in a loud voice, so that all the maidens were kept awake by thinking of the news, and by day they were being constantly reminded by all the old dueñas that the king had resolved to marry.

After the news had become somewhat stale, the question was asked, 'Who is the king going to marry?' To which the barber made reply, that probably 'he would marry a woman.'

'A woman!' exclaimed his hearers. 'Why, what else could he marry?'

'Not all women are worthy the name,' answered the barber. 'Some more resemble the unbaptized, of whom I say, abernuncio.'

'But what mean you, good friend?' demanded his customers. 'Is not the king to find a woman for wife in our land of Spain?'

'He would,' replied the barber, 'with greater ease find the

reverse; but to find a woman worthy to be his wife I shall have great trouble.'

'What, you?' exclaimed all of them. 'What have you got to do with providing the king with a wife?'

'I am under royal licence, remember,' said he of the razor; 'for I am the only man in the kingdom permitted to rub the royal features. I am the possessor of the magic mirror also, into which if any woman not being thoroughly good shall look, the blemishes on her character will appear as so many spots on its surface.'

'Is this one of the conditions?' asked all.

'This is the sole condition,' replied the barber, placing his thumbs in the armholes of his waistcoat and looking very wise.

'But is there no limit as to age?' they again inquired.

'Any woman from eighteen years upwards is eligible,' said the possessor of the mirror.

'Then you will have every woman in Granada claiming the right to be queen!' all exclaimed.

'But, first of all, they will have to justify their claim, for I will not take any woman at her word. No; she will have to gaze into the mirror with me by her side,' continued the barber.

The sole condition imposed on those who desired to become Queen of Granada was made known, and was much ridiculed, as may naturally be supposed; but, strange to say, no woman applied to the barber to have a look into the mirror.

Days and weeks went by, but the king was no nearer getting a wife. Some generous ladies would try and prevail on their lady friends to make the trial, but none seemed ambitious of the honour.

The king, be it known, was a very handsome man, and

was beloved by all his subjects for his many virtues; therefore it was surprising that none of the lovely ladies who attended court should try to become his wife.

Many excuses and explanations were given. Some were already engaged to be married, others professed themselves too proud to enter the barber's shop, while others assured their friends that they had resolved on remaining single.

The latter seem to have been cleverer in their excuses, for it was soon observable that no man in Granada would marry, assigning as a reason for this that until the king was suited they would not think of marrying; though the real cause may have been due to the objection of the ladies to look into the mirror.

The fathers of families were much annoyed at the apparent want of female ambition in their daughters, while the mothers were strangely silent on the matter.

Every morning the king would ask the barber if any young lady had ventured on looking into the mirror; but the answer was always the same—that many watched his shop to see if others went there, but none had ventured in.

'Ah, Granada, Granada!' exclaimed the king; 'hast thou no daughter to offer thy king? In this Alhambra did my predecessors enjoy the company of their wives; and am I to be denied this natural comfort?'

'Royal master,' said the barber, 'in those days the magic mirror was unknown and not so much required. Men then only studied the arts, but now is science added to their studies.'

'You mean, then,' asked the king, 'that an increase in knowledge has done no good?'

'I mean more than that,' continued the barber; 'I mean that people are worse than they used to be.'

'"God is great!" is what these walls proclaim; to know is to be wise,' urged the king.

'Not always, sir,' said the barber; 'for the majority of men and women in the present know too much and are not too wise, although some deem them wise for being cunning. There is as great a distance between wisdom and cunning as there is between the heavens and the earth.'

'Barber,' shouted the king, 'thou shalt get me a wife bright as the day, pure as dew, and good as gold—one who shall not be afraid to look into thy magic mirror!'

'Sir,' replied the barber, 'the only magic about my mirror is that which the evil consciences of the ladies of Granada conjure up. The simple shepherdess on the mountain side would brave the magic power of any mirror, strong in the consciousness of innocence; but would you marry such a lowly one?'

'Such a woman is worthy to be a queen, for she is a pearl without price,' answered the king. 'Go, bid her come here; and, in the presence of my assembled court, let the gentle shepherdess look into the mirror, after thou hast told her of the danger of so doing.'

The barber was not long in bringing the shepherdess to court with him; and it having been proclaimed throughout the city that the trial was going to be made, the principal hall was soon filled with all the grand ladies and knights of the king's household.

When the shepherdess entered the royal presence she felt very shy at being surrounded by so much grandeur; but she knew enough about her own sex to understand that they inwardly considered her not quite so ugly as they audibly expressed her to be.

The king was very much pleased with her appearance, and received her very kindly, telling her that if she desired to be his wife she would have to gaze into the magic mirror, and if she had done aught which was not consistent with her maidenly character, the mirror would show as many stains on its surface as there might be blemishes on her heart.

'Sir,' replied the maiden, 'we are all sinners in the sight of God, they say; but I am a poor shepherdess, and surrounded by my flock. I have known what it is to be loved, for, when the sheep have perceived danger, they have come to me for protection. The wild flowers have been my only ornament, the sky almost my only roof, and God my truest and best friend. Therefore, I fear not to look into that magic mirror; for although I have no ambition to become queen, yet am I not lacking in that pride which is born of the desire to be good.'

Saying which, she walked up to the mirror and gazed into it, blushing slightly, perhaps at the sight of her own beauty, which before she had only seen portrayed in the still brook.

The court ladies surrounded her; and when they saw that the magic mirror showed no stains on its surface, they snatched it from her, and exclaimed—

'There is no magic in it—a cheat has been put on us!'

But the king said—

'No, ladies; you have only yourselves to thank. Had you been as innocent as this shepherdess, who is going to be my queen, you would not have dreaded looking into the mirror.'

After the marriage the barber was heard to say, that as the magic mirror had now lost its virtue, who could tell but what this charm might be restored to Granada?

8

The Prince Who Befriended the Beasts

(Mingrelian)

There was a king, and he had three sons. Once he fell ill, and became blind in both eyes. He sent his sons for a surgeon. All the surgeons agreed that there was a fish of a rare kind by the help of which the king might be cured. They made a sketch of the fish, and left it with the sick monarch.

The king commanded his eldest son to go and catch that fish in the sea. A hundred men with their nets were lost in the sea, but nought could they find like the fish they sought. The eldest son came home to his father and said: 'I have found nothing.' This displeased the king, but what could he do? Then the second son set out, taking with him a hundred men also, but all his men were lost too, and he brought back nothing.

After this, the youngest brother went. He had recourse to cunning; he took with him a hundred kilas of flour and one man. He came to the sea, and every day he strewed flour in the water, near the shore, until all the flour was used up; the fishes grew fat on the flour, and said: 'Let us do a service to this youth since he has enabled us to grow fat'; so, as soon as the youth threw a net into the sea, he at once drew out the rare fish he sought. He wrapped it up in the skirt of his robe, and went his way.

As he rode along, some distance from his companion, he heard a voice that said: 'O youth, I am dying!' But on looking round he saw no man, and continued his journey. After a short time, he again heard the same words. He looked round more carefully, but saw nothing. Then he glanced at the skirt of his robe, and saw that the fish had its mouth open, and was dying. The youth said to it: 'What dost thou want?' The fish answered: 'It will be better for thee if thou wilt let me go, some day I shall be of use to thee.' The youth took it and threw it into the water, saying to his comrade: 'I hope thou wilt not betray me.'

When he reached home, he told his father that he had been unsuccessful. Some time passed. Once the prince quarrelled with his comrade, and the latter ran off and told the king how his son had deceived him. When the king heard this, he ordered his son to be taken away and killed. He was taken out, but when they were about to kill him, the youth entreated them, saying: 'What doth it profit you if you slay me? If you let me go, 'twill be a good deed, and I shall flee to foreign lands.' The executioners took pity on him, and set him free; he thanked them, and departed.

He went, he went, he went, he went farther than anybody ever went—he came to a great forest. As he went through the forest, he saw a deer running, in a great state of alarm. The youth stopped, and fixed his gaze on it; then the deer came up and fell on its face before him. The youth asked: 'What ails thee?' 'The prince pursues me, and on thee depends my safety.' The youth took the deer with him and went on. A huntsman met him, and asked: 'Whither art thou leading the deer?' The youth replied: 'One king has sent it as a gift to another king, and, lo! I am taking it.' The youth thus saved the deer from death, and the deer said: 'A time will come when I shall save thy life.'

The youth went on his way: he went, he went, he went, so far he went, good sir, that the 'three day colt' (of fable) could not go so far. He looked, and, lo! A frightened eagle perched on his shoulder, and said: 'Youth, on thee depends my safety!' The youth protected it also from its pursuer. Then the eagle said to him: 'Some day I shall do thee a service.'

The youth went on: he went through the forest, he went, he went, he went, he went farther than he could, he went a week, two weeks, a year and three months. Then he heard some fearful rumbling, roaring, thunder and lightning—something was coming through the forest, breaking down all the trees. A great jackal appeared, and ran up to the youth, saying: 'If thou wilt thou canst protect me; the prince is pursuing me with all his army.' The youth saved the jackal, as he had saved the other animals. Then the jackal said: 'Some day I shall help thee.'

The youth went on his way, and, when he was out of the wood, came to a town. In this town he found a castle of crystal, in the courtyard of which he saw a great number of young men, some dying and some dead. He asked the meaning of this, and was told: 'The king of this land has a daughter, a maiden queen; she has made a proclamation that she will wed him that can hide himself from her; but no man can hide himself from her, and all these men has she slain, for he that cannot hide himself from her is cast down from the top of the castle.'

When the youth heard this, he at once arose, and went to the maiden. They bowed themselves each to the other. The maiden asked him: 'Wherefore art thou come hither?' The youth answered: 'I come for that which others have come for.' She immediately called her viziers together, and they wrote out the usual contract.

The youth went out from the castle, came to the seashore, sat down, and was soon buried in thought. Just then, something made a great splash in the sea, came and swallowed the youth, carried him into the Red Sea, there they were hidden in the depths of the sea, near the shore. The youth remained there all that night.

When the maiden arose next morning she brought her mirror and looked in it, but she found nothing in the sky, she looked on the dry land, and found nothing there, she looked at the sea—and then she saw the youth in the belly of the fish, which was hiding in the deep waters. After a short time, the fish threw up the youth on the place where it had found him. He went merrily to the maiden. She asked: 'Well, then, didst thou hide thyself?' 'Yes, I hid myself.' But the maiden told him where he had been, and how he got there, and added: 'This time I forgive thee, for the cleverness thou hast shown.'

The youth set out again, and sat down in a field. Then something fell upon him, and took him up into the air, lifted him up into the sky, and covered him with its wing. When the maiden arose next morning, she looked in her mirror, she gazed at the mountain, she gazed at the earth, but she found nothing, she looked at the sky, and there she saw how the eagle was covering the youth. The eagle carried the youth down, and put him on the ground. He was joyful, thinking that the maiden could not have seen him; but when he came to her she told him all.

Then he fell into deep melancholy, but the maiden, being struck with wonder at his cunning in hiding himself, told him that she again forgave him. He went out again, and, as he was walking in the field, the deer came to him and said: 'Mount on my back.' He mounted, and the deer carried him away, away, away over all the mountains that were there, and put him in a lair. When the maiden arose next morning, she found him, and when he came back to her she said: 'Young man, it seems that thou hast many friends, but thou canst not hide thyself from me; yet this day also I forgive thee.' The youth went sadly away; he had lost confidence.

When he sat down in the field, an earthquake began, the town shook, lightning flashed, thunder rolled, and when a thunderbolt had fallen, there leapt out from it his friend the gigantic jackal, and said to him: 'Fear not, O youth!' The jackal had recourse to its wonted cunning, it began to scrape at the earth: it dug, it dug, it dug, and burrowed right up to the place where the maiden dwelt, and then it said to the youth: 'Stay thou here, she will look at the sky, the mountain, the sea, and when she cannot find thee she will break her mirror; when thou hearest this, then strike thy head through the ground and come out.'

This advice, of course, pleased the youth. When the maiden arose in the morning, she looked at the sea, she found him not, she looked at the mountain, she looked at the sky, and still she could not see him, so she broke her mirror. Then the youth pushed his head through the floor, bowed, and said to the maiden: 'Thou art mine and I am thine!' They summoned the viziers, sent the news to the king, and a great feast began.

9

Father Frost

(Russian)

In a far-away country, somewhere in Russia, there lived a stepmother who had a stepdaughter and also a daughter of her own. Her own daughter was dear to her, and always whatever she did the mother was the first to praise her, to pet her; but there was but little praise for the stepdaughter; although good and kind, she had no other reward than reproach. What on earth could have been done? The wind blows, but stops blowing at times; the wicked woman never knows how to stop her wickedness. One bright cold day the stepmother said to her husband:

'Now, old man, I want thee to take thy daughter away from my eyes, away from my ears. Thou shalt not take her to thy people into a warm izba. Thou shalt take her into the wide, wide fields to the crackling frost.'

The old father grew sad, began even to weep, but nevertheless helped the young girl into the sleigh. He wished to cover her with a sheepskin in order to protect her from the cold; however, he did not do it. He was afraid; his wife was watching them out of the window. And so he went with his lovely daughter into the wide, wide fields; drove her nearly to the woods, left her there alone, and speedily drove away—he was a good man and did not care to see his daughter's death.

Alone, quite alone, remained the sweet girl. Broken-hearted and terror-stricken she repeated fervently all the prayers she knew.

Father Frost, the almighty sovereign at that place, clad in furs, with a long, long, white beard and a shining crown on his white head, approached nearer and nearer, looked at this beautiful guest of his and asked:

'Dost thou know me?—me, the red-nosed Frost?'

'Be welcome, Father Frost,' answered gently the young girl. 'I hope our heavenly Lord sent thee for my sinful soul.'

'Art thou comfortable, sweet child?' again asked the Frost. He was exceedingly pleased with her looks and mild manners.

'Indeed I am,' answered the girl, almost out of breath from cold.

And the Frost, cheerful and bright, kept crackling in the branches until the air became icy, but the good-natured girl kept repeating:

'I am very comfortable, dear Father Frost.'

But the Frost, however, knew all about the weakness of human beings; he knew very well that few of them are really good and kind; but he knew no one of them even could struggle too long against the power of Frost, the king of winter. The kindness of the gentle girl charmed old Frost so much that he made the decision to treat her differently from others, and gave her a large heavy trunk filled with many beautiful, beautiful things. He gave her a rich 'schouba' lined with precious furs; he gave her silk quilts—light like feathers and warm as a mother's lap. What a rich girl she became and how many magnificent garments she received! And besides all, old Frost gave her a blue 'sarafan' ornamented with silver and pearls.

'Old Frost gave the gentle girl many beautiful, beautiful things.'

When the young girl put it on she became such a beautiful maiden that even the sun smiled at her.

The stepmother was in the kitchen busy baking pancakes for the meal which it is the custom to give to the priests and friends after the usual service for the dead.

'Now, old man,' said the wife to the husband, 'go down to the wide fields and bring the body of thy daughter; we will bury her.'

The old man went off. And the little dog in the corner wagged his tail and said:

'Bow-wow! bow-wow! The old man's daughter is on her way home, beautiful and happy as never before, and the old woman's daughter is wicked as ever before.'

'Keep still, stupid beast!' shouted the stepmother, and struck the little dog.

'Here, take this pancake, eat it and say, "The old woman's daughter will be married soon and the old man's daughter shall be buried soon."'

The dog ate the pancake and began anew:

'Bow-wow! bow-wow! The old man's daughter is coming home wealthy and happy as never before, and the old woman's daughter is somewhere around as homely and wicked as ever before.'

The old woman was furious at the dog, but in spite of pancakes and whipping, the dog repeated the same words over and over again.

Somebody opened the gate, voices were heard laughing and

talking outside. The old woman looked out and sat down in amazement. The stepdaughter was there like a princess, bright and happy in the most beautiful garments, and behind her the old father had hardly strength enough to carry the heavy, heavy trunk with the rich outfit.

'Old man!' called the stepmother, impatiently; 'hitch our best horses to our best sleigh, and drive my daughter to the very same place in the wide, wide fields.'

The old man obeyed as usual and took his stepdaughter to the same place and left her alone.

Old Frost was there; he looked at his new guest.

'Art thou comfortable, fair maiden?' asked the red-nosed sovereign.

'Let me alone,' harshly answered the girl; 'canst thou not see that my feet and my hands are about stiff from the cold?'

The Frost kept crackling and asking questions for quite a while, but obtaining no polite answer became angry and froze the girl to death.

'Old man, go for my daughter; take the best horses; be careful; do not upset the sleigh; do not lose the trunk.'

And the little dog in the corner said:

'Bow-wow! Bow-wow! The old man's daughter will marry soon; the old woman's daughter shall be buried soon.'

'Do not lie. Here is a cake; eat it and say, "The old woman's daughter is clad in silver and gold."'

The gate opened, the old woman ran out and kissed the stiff frozen lips of her daughter. She wept and wept, but there was no help, and she understood at last that through her own wickedness and envy her child had perished.

10

The Goddess Who Came to Live with Mankind

(Indian, Khasi)

Shillong Peak is the highest mountain in the Khasi Hills, and although it bears such a prosaic name in our days, the mountain was a place of renown in the days of the Ancient Khasis, full of romance and mystery, sacred to the spirits and to the gods. In those days the mountain itself, and the whole country to the north of it, was one vast forest, where dwelt demons and dragons, who cast evil spells and caused dire sickness to fall upon any unfortunate person who happened to spend a night in that wild forest.

In the mountain there lived a god. At first the Ancients had no clear revelation about this deity; they were vaguely aware of his existence, but there was no decree that sacrifices should be offered to him. After a time there arose among the Khasis a very wise man of the name of U Shillong who was endowed with great insight to understand the mysteries, and he discovered that the god of the mountain was great and powerful, and sacrifice and reverence should be offered to him, and he taught his neighbours how to perform the rites acceptably. The name of the deity was not revealed, so the people began to call him

'U 'Lei Shillong' (the god of U Shillong) after the name of the man who first paid him homage. Then gradually he came to be called 'the god Shillong,' and in time the mountain itself was called the mountain of Shillong, and from this is derived the name of the present town of Shillong.

Possibly the god Shillong was, and remains, one of the best-known and most generally reverenced of all the Khasi gods, for even on the far hill-tops of Jaintia altars have been raised to his service and honour. Although sacrifices are being offered to him at distant shrines, the abode of the god is in the Shillong mountain, more especially in the sacred grove on the summit of the peak itself, which is such a familiar landmark in the country.

Judging from tradition, this deity was regarded as a benign and benevolent being, forbearing in his attitude towards mankind, who were privileged to hunt in his forests unhindered by dangers and sicknesses, and the dances of mankind were acceptable in his sight. He frequently assisted them in their misfortunes and helped them to overcome the oppression of demons. It was he who endowed U Suidnoh with wisdom to fight and to conquer U Thlen, the great snake-god and vampire from Cherrapoonjee, and it was by his intervention that Ka Thei and her sister were delivered from the grasp of the merciless demon, U Ksuid Tynjang.

Tradition also points out that this famous deity had a wife and family, and three at least of his daughters are renowned in Khasi folk-lore. One of them transformed herself into the likeness of a Khasi maiden and came to live with mankind, where she became the ancestress of a race of chiefs. Two other daughters, out of playfulness, transformed themselves into two rivers, and are with us in that form to this day. This is the story of the goddess who came to live with mankind:

Many hundreds of years ago, near the place now known as Pomlakrai, there was a cave called the Cave of Marai, near to which stood a high perpendicular rock around which the youthful cow-herds of the time used to play. They gathered there from different directions, and passed the time merrily, practising archery and playing on their flutes, while keeping an eye on their herds. The rock was too high for them to attempt to climb it, and it was always spoken of as 'the rock on which the foot of man never trod.'

On a certain day, when the lads came as usual to the familiar rendezvous, they were surprised to see, sitting on the top of the rock, a fair young girl watching them silently and wistfully. The children, being superstitious, took fright at sight of her and ran in terror to Mylliem, their village, leaving the cattle to shift for themselves. When they told their news, the whole village was roused and men quickly gathered to the public meeting-place to hold a consultation. They decided to go and see for themselves if the apparition seen by the children was a real live child, or if they had been deluded by some spell or enchantment. Under the guidance of the lads, they hurried to the place on the hill where the rock stood, and there, as the boys had stated, sat a fair and beautiful child.

The clothes worn by the little girl were far richer than any worn by their own women-folk, so they judged that she belonged to some rich family, and she was altogether so lovely that the men gazed open-mouthed at her, dazzled by her beauty. Their sense of chivalry soon asserted itself, however, and they began to devise plans to rescue the maiden from her perilous position.

To climb up the face of that steep rock was an impossible feat; so they called to her, but she would not answer; they made signs for her to descend, but she did not stir, and the men felt baffled and perplexed.

Chief among the rescuers was a man called U Mylliem Ngap, who was remarkable for his sagacity and courage. When he saw that the child refused to be coaxed, he attributed it to her fear to venture unaided down that steep and slippery rock. So he sent some of his comrades to the jungle to cut down some bamboos, which he joined together and made into a pole long enough to reach the top of the rock. Then he beckoned to the child to take hold of it, but she sat on unmoved.

By this time the day was beginning to wane, yet the child did not stir and the rescuers were growing desperate. To leave her to her fate on that impregnable rock would be little less than cold-blooded murder, for nothing but death awaited her. They began to lament loudly, as people lament when mourning for their dead, but the child sat on in the same indifferent attitude.

Just then U Mylliem Ngap noticed a tuft of wild flowers growing near the cave, and he quickly gathered a bunch and fastened it to the end of the long pole and held it up to the maiden's view. The moment she saw the flowers, she gave a cry of delight and held out her hand to take them. U Mylliem Ngap promptly lowered the pole and the child moved towards it, but before she could grasp the flowers the pole was again lowered; so, little by little, step by step, as the men watched with bated breath, the little maid reached the ground in safety.

U Mylliem Ngap, with general consent, constituted himself her champion. He called her 'Pah Syntiew', which means 'Lured by Flowers', for her name and her origin were unknown. He took her to his own home and adopted her as his own daughter, cherishing her with fondness and affection, which the child fully requited.

Ka Pah Syntiew, as she grew up, fulfilled all the promises of her childhood and developed into a woman of incomparable beauty and her fame went abroad throughout the country. She was also gifted and wise beyond all the maidens of the neighbourhood, and was the chosen leader at all the Khasi dances and festivals. She taught the Khasi girls to dance and to sing, and it was she who instituted the Virgins' Dance, which remains popular to this day among the Khasis. Her foster-father, seeing she possessed so much discretion and wisdom, used to consult her in all his perplexities and seek her advice in all matters pertaining to the ruling of the village. She displayed such tact and judgement that people from other villages brought their disputes to her to be settled, and she was acknowledged to be wiser and more just than any ruler in the country, and they began to call her 'Ka Siem' (the Chiefess, or the Queen).

When she came of age, U Mylliem Ngap gave her in marriage to a man of prowess and worth, who is mentioned in Khasi lore as 'U Kongor Nongjri.' She became the mother of many sons and daughters, who were all noble and comely.

After her children had grown up, Ka Pah Syntiew called them all to her one day and revealed to them the secret of her birth. She was the daughter of U 'Lei Shillong, the mountain god, permitted by her father to dwell for a period among mankind, and at last the time was at hand for her to return to her native element.

Not long after this Ka Pah Syntiew walked away in the direction of the cave of Marai, and no one dared to accompany her, for it was realized that her hour of departure had come. From that day she disappeared from mortal ken. Her descendants are known to this day as two of the leading families of Khasi chiefs, or Siems, and in common parlance these two families, those of Khairim and Mylliem, are still called 'the Siems (the Chiefs) of Shillong', or 'the Siems of the god'.

11

The Wolf-Child

(Spanish/Portuguese)

In the North of Portugal there are many sequestered spots where the enchanted Moors and the wizards meet when it is full moon. These places are generally situated among high rocks on the precipitous sides of the hills overlooking rivers; and when the wind is very boisterous their terrible screams and incantations can be distinctly heard by the peasantry inhabiting the neighbouring villages.

On such occasions the father of the family sets fire to a wisp of straw, and with it makes the sign of the cross around his house, which prevents these evil spirits from approaching. The other members of the family place a few extra lights before the image of the Virgin; and the horse-shoe nailed to the door completes the safety of the house.

But it will so happen that sometimes an enchanted Moor, with more cunning than honesty, will get through one of the windows on the birth of a child, and will brand the infant with the crescent on his shoulder or arm, in which case it is well known that the child, on certain nights, will be changed into a wolf.

The enchanted Moors have their castles and palaces under

the ground or beneath the rivers, and they wander about the earth, seeing but not seen; for they died unbaptized, and have, therefore, no rest in the grave.

They seem to have given preference to the North of Portugal, where they are held in great fear by the ignorant peasantry; and it has been observed that all such of the natives as have left their homes to study at the universities, on their return have never been visited by the enchanted Moors, as it is well known that they have a great respect for learning. In fact, one of the kings has said that until all his subjects were educated they would never get rid of the enchanted Moors and wizards.

In a village called Darque, on the banks of the Lima, there lived a farmer whose goodness and ignorance were only equalled by those of his wife. They were both young and robust, and were sufficiently well off to afford the luxury of beef once or twice a month. Their clothes were home-spun, and their hearts were homely. Beyond their landlord's grounds they had never stepped; but as he owned nearly the whole village, it is very evident that they knew something of this world of ours. They were both born and married on the estate, as their parents had been before them, and they were contented because they had never mixed with the world.

One day, when the farmer came home to have his midday meal of broth and maize bread, he found his wife in bed with a newborn baby boy by her side, and he was so pleased that he spent his hour of rest looking at the child, so that his meal remained untasted on the table.

Kissing his wife and infant, and bidding her beware of evil eyes, he hurried out of the house back to his work; and so great was his joy at being a father that he did not feel hungry.

He was digging potatoes, and in his excitement had sent his hoe through some of them, which, however, he did not notice until he happened to strike one that was so hard that the steel of his hoe flashed.

Thinking it was a pebble, he stooped to pick it up, but was surprised to see that it was no longer there.

However, he went on working, when he struck another hard potato, and his hoe again flashed.

'Ah,' said he, 'the evil one has been sowing this field with stones, as he did in the days of good Saint Euphemia, our patroness.' Saying which, he drew out the small crucifix from under his shirt, and the flinty potato disappeared; but he noticed that one of its eyes moved.

He thought no more of this untoward event, and went on hoeing until sunset, when, with the other labourers, he shouldered his hoe and prepared to go home.

Never had the distance seemed so great; but at last he found himself by his wife's bedside. She told him that while he was absent an old woman had called, asking for something to eat, and that as she seemed to have met with some accident, because there was blood running down her face, she invited her in, and told her she might eat what her husband had left untasted.

Sitting down at the table, the old woman commenced eating without asking a blessing on the food; and when she had finished she approached the bed, and, looking at the infant, she muttered some words and left the house hurriedly.

The husband and wife were very much afraid that the old woman was a witch; but as the child went on growing and seemed well they gradually forgot their visitor.

The infant was baptized, and was named John; and when

he was old enough he was sent out to work to help his parents. All the labourers noticed that John could get through more work than any man, he was so strong and active; but he was very silent.

The remarkable strength of the boy got to be so spoken about in the village that at last the wise woman, who was always consulted, said that there was no doubt but that John was a wolf-child; and this having come to the ears of his parents, his body was carefully examined, and the mark of the crescent was found under his arm.

Nothing now remained to be done but to take John to the great wise woman of Arifana, and have him disenchanted.

The day had arrived for the parents to take John with them to Arifana, but when they looked for him he could nowhere be found. They searched everywhere—down the well, in the river, in the forest—and made inquiries at all the villages, but in vain; John had disappeared.

Weeks went by without any sign of him; and the winter having set in, the wolves, through hunger, had become more undaunted in their attacks on the flocks and herds. The farmer, afraid of firing at them, lest he might shoot his son, had laid a trap; and one morning, to his delight, he saw that a very large wolf had been caught, which one of his fellow-labourers was cudgelling. Fearing it might be the lost wolf-child, he hastened to the spot, and prevented the wolf receiving more blows; but it was too late, apparently, to save the creature's life, for it lay motionless on the ground as if dead. Hurrying off for the wise woman of the village, she returned with him; and, close to the head of the wolf, she gathered some branches of the common pine-tree, and lighting them, as some were green and others dry, a volume of smoke arose like a tower, reaching to the top of a hill where lived some notorious enchanted Moors and wizards; so that between the wolf and the said Moors the distance was covered by a tunnel of smoke and fire. Then the wise woman intoned the following words, closing her eyes, and bidding the rest do so until she should tell them they might open them:—

> 'Spirit of the mighty wind
> That across the desert howls,
> Help us here to unbind
> All the spells of dreaded ghouls;
>
> Through the path of smoke and fire
> Rising to the wizards' mound,
> Bid the cursèd mark retire
> From this creature on the ground;
> Bid him take his shape again,
> Free him from the Crescent's power,
> May the holy Cross remain
> On his temple from this hour.'

She now made the sign of the Cross over the head of the wolf, and continued:—

> 'River, winding to the west,
> Stay thy rippling current, stay,
> Jordan's stream thy tide has blest,
> Help us wash this stain away;
> Bear it to the ocean wide,
> Back to Saracenic shore.
> Those who washed in thee have died
> But to live for evermore.'

Then she sprinkled a few drops over the fire, which caused a larger amount of smoke, and exclaimed—

> 'Hie thee, spirit, up through smoke,
> Quenched by water and by fire;
> Hie thee far from Christian folk,
> To the wizard's home retire.
> Open wide your eyelids now,
> All the smoke has curled away;
> 'Neath the peaceful olive bough
> Let us go, and let us pray.'

Then they all rose, and the wolf was no longer there. The fire had burned itself out, and the stream was again running. In slow procession they went to the olive grotto, headed by the wise woman; and, after praying, they returned to the house, where they found, to their delight, John fast asleep in his bed; but his arms showed signs of bruises which had been caused by the cudgelling he had received when he was caught in the trap.

There were great rejoicings that day in the village of Darque; and no one was better pleased than John at having regained his proper shape.

He was never known to join in the inhuman sport of hunting wolves for pleasure, because, as he said, although they may not be wolf-children, they do but obey an instinct which was given them; and to be kind-hearted is to obey a precept which was given us. And, owing to the introduction into Portugal of the Book in which this commandment is to be found, wolf-children have become scarcer, and the people wiser.

12

How Wisdom Became the Property of the Human Race

(West African)

There once lived, in Fanti-land, a man named Father Anansi. He possessed all the wisdom in the world. People came to him daily for advice and help.

One day the men of the country were unfortunate enough to offend Father Anansi, who immediately resolved to punish them. After much thought he decided that the severest penalty he could inflict would be to hide all his wisdom from them. He set to work at once to gather again all that he had already given. When he had succeeded, as he thought, in collecting it, he placed all in one great pot. This he carefully sealed, and determined to put it in a spot where no human being could reach it.

Now, Father Anansi had a son, whose name was Kweku Tsin. This boy began to suspect his father of some secret design, so he made up his mind to watch carefully. Next day he saw his father quietly slip out of the house, with his precious pot hung round his neck. Kweku Tsin followed. Father Anansi went through the forest till he had left the village far behind. Then, selecting the highest and most inaccessible-looking tree, he began to climb. The heavy pot, hanging in front of him, made his ascent almost impossible. Again and again he tried to reach the top of the tree, where he intended to hang the pot. There, he thought, Wisdom would indeed be beyond the reach of every one but himself. He was unable, however, to carry out his desire. At each trial the pot swung in his way.

For some time Kweku Tsin watched his father's vain attempts. At last, unable to contain himself any longer, he cried out: 'Father, why do you not hang the pot on your back? Then you could easily climb the tree.'

Father Anansi turned and said: 'I thought I had all the world's wisdom in this pot. But I find you possess more than I do. All my wisdom was insufficient to show me what to do, yet you have been able to tell me.' In his anger he threw the pot down. It struck on a great rock and broke. The wisdom contained in it escaped and spread throughout the world.

13

The Man with His Leg Tied Up

(Native American)

As a punishment for having once upon a time used that foot against a venerable medicine man, Aggo Dah Gauda had one leg looped up to his thigh, so that he was obliged to get along by hopping. By dint of practice he had become very skillful in this exercise, and he could make leaps which seemed almost incredible.

Aggo had a beautiful daughter, and his chief care was to secure her from being carried off by the king of the buffalos, who was the ruler of all the herds of that kind, and had them entirely at his command to make them do as he willed.

Dah Gauda, too, was quite an important person in his own way, for he lived in great state, having a log house of his own, and a court-yard which extended from the sill of his front-door as many hundred miles westward as he chose to measure it.

Although he might claim this extensive privilege of ground, he advised his daughter to keep within doors, and by no means to go far in the neighbourhood, as she would otherwise be sure to be stolen away, as he was satisfied that the buffalo-king spent night and day lurking about and lying in wait to seize her.

One sunshiny morning, when there were just two or three promising clouds rolling moistly about the sky, Aggo prepared to go out a-fishing; but before he left the lodge he reminded her of her strange and industrious lover, whom she had never seen.

'My daughter,' said he, 'I am going out to fish, and as the day will be a pleasant one, you must recollect that we have an enemy near, who is constantly going about with two eyes that never close, and do not expose yourself out of the lodge.'

With this excellent advice, Aggo hopped off in high spirits; but he had scarcely reached the fishing-ground when he heard a voice singing, at a distance:

Man with the leg tied up,
Man with the leg tied up,
Broken hip—hip—
Hipped.
Man with the leg tied up,
Man with the leg tied up,
Broken leg—leg—
Legged.

There was no one in sight, but Aggo heard the words quite plainly, and as he suspected the ditty to be the work of his enemies, the buffalos, he hopped home as fast as his one leg could carry him.

Meantime, the daughter had no sooner been left alone in the lodge than she thought with herself:

'It is hard to be thus forever kept in doors. But my father says it would be dangerous to venture abroad. I know what I will do. I will get on the top of the house, and there I can comb and dress my hair, and no one can harm me.'

She accordingly ascended the roof and busied herself in untying and combing her beautiful hair; for it was truly beautiful, not only of a fine, glossy quality, but it was so very long that it hung over the eaves of the house and reached down on the ground, as she sat dressing it.

She was wholly occupied in this employment, without a thought of danger, when, all of a sudden, the king of the buffalos came dashing on with his herd of followers, and making sure of her by means of her drooping tresses, he placed her upon the back of one of his favourite buffalos, and away he cantered over the plains. Plunging into a river that bounded his land, he bore her safely to his lodge on the other side.

And now the buffalo-king having secured the beautiful person of Aggo Dah Gauda's daughter, he set to work to make her heart his own—a little ceremony which it would have been, perhaps, wiser for his majesty, the king of the buffalos, to have attended to before, for he now worked to little purpose. Although he laboured with great zeal to gain her affections, she sat pensive and disconsolate in the lodge, among the other females, and scarcely ever spoke, nor did she take the least interest in the affairs of the king's household.

To the king himself she paid no heed, and although he breathed forth to her every soft and gentle word he could think of, she sat still and motionless for all the world like one of the lowly bushes by the door of her father's lodge, when the summer wind has died away.

The king enjoined it upon the others in the lodge as a special edict, on pain of instant death, to give to Aggo's daughter every thing that she wanted, and to be careful not to displease her. They set before her the choicest food. They gave her the seat of honour in the lodge. The king himself went out hunting to obtain the most dainty meats, both of animals and wild fowl, to pleasure her palate; and he treated her every morning to a ride upon one of the royal buffalos, who was so gentle in his motions as not even to disturb a single one of the tresses of the beautiful hair of Aggo's daughter as she paced along.

And not content with these proofs of his attachment, the king would sometimes fast from all food, and having thus purified his spirit and cleared his voice, he would take his Indian flute, and, sitting before the lodge, give vent to his feelings in pensive echoes, something after this fashion:

My sweetheart,
My sweetheart,
Ah me!
When I think of you,
When I think of you,
Ah me!
What can I do, do, do?
How I love you,
How I love you,
Ah me!
Do not hate me,
Do not hate me,
Ah me!
Speak—e'en berate me.

When I think of you,
Ah me!
What can I do, do, do?

In the mean time, Aggo Dah Gauda had reached home, and finding that his daughter had been stolen, his indignation was so thoroughly awakened that he would have forthwith torn every hair from his head, but, being entirely bald, this was out of the question, so, as an easy and natural vent to his feelings, Aggo hopped off half a mile in every direction. First he hopped east, then he hopped west, next he hopped north, and again he hopped south, all in search of his daughter; till the one leg was fairly tired out. Then he sat down in his lodge, and resting himself a little, he reflected, and then he vowed that his single leg should never know rest again until he had found his beautiful daughter and brought her home. For this purpose he immediately set out.

Now that he proceeded more coolly, he could easily track the buffalo-king until he came to the banks of the river, where he saw that he had plunged in and swam over. There having been a frosty night or two since, the water was so covered with thin ice that Aggo could not venture upon it, even with one leg. He encamped hard by till it became more solid, and then crossed over and pursued the trail.

As he went along he saw branches broken off and strewed behind, which guided him in his course; for these had been purposely cast along by the daughter. And the manner in which she had accomplished it was this. Her hair was all untied when she was caught up, and being very long it took hold of the branches as they darted along, and it was these twigs that she broke off as signs to her father.

When Aggo came to the king's lodge it was evening. Carefully approaching, he peeped through the sides, and saw his daughter sitting disconsolate. She immediately caught his eye, and knowing that it was her father come for her, she all at once appeared to relent in her heart, and, asking for the royal dipper, said to the king, 'I will go and get you a drink of water.'

This token of submission delighted his majesty, and, high in hope, he waited with impatience for her return.

At last he went out, but nothing could be seen or heard of the captive daughter. Calling together his followers, they sallied forth upon the plains, and had not gone far when they espied by the light of the moon, which was shining roundly just over the edge of the prairie, Aggo Dah Gauda, his daughter in his arms, making all speed with his one leg toward the west.

The buffalos being set on by their king, raised a great shout, and scampered off in pursuit. They thought to overtake Aggo in less than no time; but although he had a single leg only, it was in such fine condition to go, that to every pace of theirs, he hopped the length of a cedar-tree.

But the buffalo-king was well assured that he would be able to overtake Aggo, hop as briskly as he might. It would be a mortal shame, thought the king, to be outstripped by a man with one leg tied up; so, shouting and cheering, and issuing orders on all sides, he set the swiftest of his herd upon the track, with strict commands to take Aggo dead or alive. And a curious sight it was to see.

At one time a buffalo would gain handsomely upon Aggo, and be just at the point of laying hold of him, when off Aggo would hop, a good furlong, in an oblique line, wide out of his reach; which bringing him nearly in contact with another of the herd, away he would go again, just as far off in another direction.

And in this way Aggo kept the whole company of the buffalos zig-zagging across the plain, with the poor king at their head, running to and fro, shouting among them and hurrying them about in the wildest way. It was an extraordinary road that Aggo was taking toward home; and after a time it so puzzled and bewildered the buffalos that they were driven half out of their wits, and they roared, and brandished their tails, and foamed, as if they would put out of countenance and frighten out of sight the old man in the moon, who was looking on all the time, just above the edge of the prairie.

As for the king himself, losing at last all patience at the absurd idea of chasing a man with one leg all night long, he called his herd together, and fled, in disgust, toward the west, and never more appeared in all that part of the country.

Aggo, relieved of his pursuers, hopped off a hundred steps in one, till he reached the stream, crossed it in a twinkling of the eye, and bore his daughter in triumph to his lodge.

In the course of time Aggo's beautiful daughter married a very worthy young warrior, who was neither a buffalo-king nor so much as the owner of any more of the buffalos than a splendid skin robe which he wore, with great effect, thrown over his shoulders, on his wedding-day. On which occasion, Aggo Dah Gauda hopped about on his one leg livelier than ever.

14

Crocodile's Treason

(South African)

Crocodile was, in the days when animals still could talk, the acknowledged foreman of all water creatures and if one should judge from appearances one would say that he still is. But in those days it was his especial duty to have a general care of all water animals, and when one year it was exceedingly dry, and the water of the river where they had lived dried up and became scarce, he was forced to make a plan to trek over to another river a short distance from there.

He first sent Otter out to spy. He stayed away two days and brought back a report that there was still good water in the other river, real sea-cow holes, that not even a drought of several years could dry up.

After he had ascertained this, Crocodile called to his side Tortoise and Alligator.

'Look here,' said he, 'I need you two to-night to carry a report to Lion. So then get ready; the veldt is dry, and you will probably have to travel for a few days without any water. We must make peace with Lion and his subjects, otherwise we utterly perish this year. And he must help us to trek over to the other river, especially past the Boer's farm that lies in between, and to travel unmolested by any of the animals of the veldt, so long as the trek lasts. A fish on land is sometimes a very helpless thing, as you all know.' The two had it mighty hard in the burning sun, and on the dry veldt, but eventually they reached Lion and handed him the treaty.

'What is going on now?' thought Lion to himself, when he had read it. 'I must consult Jackal first,' said he. But to the commissioners he gave back an answer that he would be the following evening with his advisers at the appointed place, at the big vaarland willow tree, at the farther end of the hole of water, where Crocodile had his headquarters.

When Tortoise and Alligator came back, Crocodile was exceedingly pleased with himself at the turn the case had taken.

He allowed Otter and a few others to be present and ordered them on that evening to have ready plenty of fish and other eatables for their guests under the vaarland willow.

That evening as it grew dark Lion appeared with Wolf, Jackal, Baboon, and a few other important animals, at the appointed place, and they were received in the most open-hearted manner by Crocodile and the other water creatures.

Crocodile was so glad at the meeting of the animals that he now and then let fall a great tear of joy that disappeared into the sand. After the other animals had done well by the fish, Crocodile laid bare to them the condition of affairs and opened up his plan. He wanted only peace among all animals; for they not only destroyed one another, but the Boer, too, would in time destroy them all.

The Boer had already stationed at the source of the river no less than three steam pumps to irrigate his land, and the water was becoming scarcer every day. More than this, he took advantage of their unfortunate position by making them sit in the shallow water and then, one after the other, bringing about their death. As Lion was, on this account, inclined to make peace, it was to his glory to take this opportunity and give his hand to these peace-making water creatures, and carry out their part of the contract, namely, escort them from the dried-up water, past the Boer's farm and to the long sea-cow pools.

'And what benefit shall we receive from it?' asked Jackal.

'Well,' answered Crocodile, 'the peace made is of great benefit to both sides. We will not exterminate each other. If you desire to come and drink water, you can do so with an easy mind, and not be the least bit nervous that I, or any one of us will seize you by the nose; and so also with all the other animals. And from your side we are to be freed from Elephant, who has the habit, whenever he gets the opportunity, of tossing us with his trunk up into some open and narrow fork of a tree and there allowing us to become biltong.'

Lion and Jackal stepped aside to consult with one another, and then Lion wanted to know what form of security he would have that Crocodile would keep to his part of the contract.

'I stake my word of honour,' was the prompt answer from Crocodile, and he let drop a few more long tears of honesty into the sand.

Baboon then said it was all square and honest as far as he could see into the case. He thought it was nonsense to attempt to dig pitfalls for one another; because he personally was well aware that his race would benefit somewhat from this contract of peace and friendship. And more than this, they must consider that use must be made of the fast disappearing water, for even in the best of times it was an unpleasant thing to be always carrying your life about in your hands. He would, however, like to suggest to the King that it would be well to have everything put down in writing, so that there would be nothing to regret in case it was needed.

Jackal did not want to listen to the agreement. He could not see that it would benefit the animals of the veldt. But Wolf, who had fully satisfied himself with the fish, was in an exceptionally peace-loving mood, and he advised Lion again to close the agreement.

After Lion had listened to all his advisers, and also the pleading tones of Crocodile's followers, he held forth in a speech in which he said that he was inclined to enter into the agreement, seeing that it was clear that Crocodile and his subjects were in a very tight place.

There and then a document was drawn up, and it was resolved, before midnight, to begin the trek. Crocodile's messengers swam in all directions to summon together the water animals for the trek.

Frogs croaked and crickets chirped in the long water grass. It was not long before all the animals had assembled at the vaarland willow. In the meantime Lion had sent out a few despatch riders to his subjects to raise a commando for an escort, and long ere midnight these also were at the vaarland willow in the moonlight.

The trek then was regulated by Lion and Jackal. Jackal was to take the lead to act as spy, and when he was able to draw Lion to one side, he said to him:

'See here, I do not trust this affair one bit, and I want to tell you straight out, I am going to make tracks! I will spy for you until you reach the sea-cow pool, but I am not going to be the one to await your arrival there.'

Elephant had to act as advance guard because he could walk so softly and could hear and smell so well. Then came Lion with one division of the animals, then Crocodile's trek with a flank protection of both sides, and Wolf received orders to bring up the rear.

Meanwhile, while all this was being arranged, Crocodile was smoothly preparing his treason. He called Yellow Snake to one side and said to him: 'It is to our advantage to have these animals, who go among us every day, and who will continue to do so, fall into the hands of the Boer. Listen, now! You remain behind unnoticed, and when you hear me shout you will know that we have arrived safely at the sea-cow pool. Then you must harass the Boer's dogs as much as you can, and the rest will look out for themselves.'

Thereupon the trek moved on. It was necessary to go very slowly as many of the water animals were not accustomed to the journey on land; but they trekked past the Boer's farm in safety, and toward break of day they were all safely at the sea-cow pool. There most of the water animals disappeared suddenly into the deep water, and Crocodile also began to make preparations to follow their example. With tearful eyes he said to Lion that he was, oh, so thankful for the help, that, from pure relief and joy, he must first give vent to his feelings by a few screams. Thereupon he suited his words to actions so that even the mountains echoed, and then thanked Lion on behalf of his subjects, and purposely continued with a long speech, dwelling on all the benefits both sides would derive from the agreement of peace.

Lion was just about to say good day and take his departure, when the first shot fell, and with it Elephant and a few other animals.

'I told you all so!' shouted Jackal from the other side of the sea-cow pool. 'Why did you allow yourselves to be misled by a few Crocodile tears?'

Crocodile had disappeared long ago into the water. All one saw was just a lot of bubbles; and on the banks there was an actual war against the animals. It simply crackled the way the Boers shot them.

But most of them, fortunately, came out of it alive.

Shortly after, they say, Crocodile received his well-earned reward, when he met a driver with a load of dynamite. And even now when the Elephant gets the chance he pitches them up into the highest forks of the trees.

15

Two Brothers

(Georgian)

Once upon a time there were two brothers. Each of them possessed ten loaves of bread, and they said: 'Let us go and seek our fortune.' So they arose and went forth.

When they had gone a little way, they were hungry. One brother said to the other: 'Come, let us eat thy bread first, then we can eat mine.' And he agreed, and they took of his loaves and did eat, and they afterwards went on their way. And they travelled for some time in this manner.

At last, when these ten loaves were finished, the brother who had first spoken said: 'Now, my brother, thou canst go thy way and I shall go mine. Thou hast no loaves left, and I will not let thee eat my bread.' So saying, he left him to continue his journey alone.

He went on and on, and came to a mill in a thick forest. He saw the miller and said: 'For the love of God, let me stay here to-night.'

The miller answered: 'Brother, it is a very terrible thing to be here at night; as thou seest, even I go elsewhere. Presently wild beasts will assemble in the wood and probably come here.'

'Have no fear for me; I shall stay here. The beasts cannot kill me,' answered the boy.

The miller tried to persuade him not to endanger his life, but when he found his arguments were of no avail, he rose and went home. The boy crept inside the hopper of the mill.

There appeared, from no one knows where, a big bear; he was followed by a wolf, and then a jackal, and they all made a great noise in the mill. They leaped and bounded just as if they were having a dance. He was terrified and, trembling from fear, he lay down, quaking all over, in the hopper.

At last the bear said: 'Come, let each of us tell something he has seen or heard.'

'We shall tell our tales, but you must begin,' cried his companions.

The bear said: 'Well, on a hill that I know, dwells a mouse. This mouse has a great heap of money, which it spreads out when the sun shines. If anyone knew of this mouse's hole and went there on a sunny day, when the money is spread out, and struck the mouse with a twig and killed it, he would become possessed of great wealth.'

'That is not wonderful!' said the wolf. 'I know a certain town where there is no water, and every mouthful has to be carried a great distance, and an enormous price is paid for it! The inhabitants do not know that in the centre of their town, under a certain stone, is beautiful, pure water. Now, if any one knew of this and would roll away that stone, he would obtain great wealth.'

'That is nothing,' said the jackal. 'I know of a king who has one only daughter, and she has been an invalid for three years. Quite a simple remedy would cure her: if she were bathed in a bath of beech leaves she would be healed. You have no idea what a fortune any one would get if he only knew this.'

When they had spoken thus, day began to dawn. The bear, the wolf, and the jackal went away into the wood. The boy came out of the hopper, gave thanks to God, and went to the mouse's hole of which the bear had spoken.

He arrived and saw that the story was true. There was the mouse with the money spread out. He stole up noiselessly and, taking twigs in his hand, he struck the mouse until he had killed it and then gathered up the money.

Then he went to the waterless town, rolled away the stone, and behold! Streams of water flowed forth. He received a reward for this and set out for the kingdom of which the jackal had spoken.

He arrived and enquired of the king: 'What wilt thou give me if I cure thy daughter?'

The king replied: 'If thou canst do this I will give thee my daughter to wife.'

The youth prepared the remedy, made the princess bathe in it, and she was cured. The king rejoiced greatly, gave him the maiden in marriage, and appointed him heir to the kingdom.

This story reached the ears of the youth's brother. He went on and on, and it came to pass that he found his brother. He asked him: 'How and by what cunning has this happened?'

The fortunate youth told him all in detail.

'I also shall go and stay at that mill a night or two.' His brother used many entreaties to dissuade him and, when he would not listen, said: 'Well, go if thou wilt, but I warn thee again it is very dangerous.'

However, he would not be persuaded and went away. He crept into the hopper and was there all night.

From some place or other arrived the former guests—the bear, the wolf, and the jackal.

The bear said: 'That day when I told you my story, the mouse was killed, and the money all taken away.'

The wolf said: 'And the stone was rolled away in the waterless town of which I spoke.'

'And the king's daughter was cured,' added the jackal.

'Then perhaps someone was listening when we talked here,' said the bear.

'Perhaps someone is here now,' shrieked his companions.

'Then let us go and look; certainly no one shall listen again,' said the three, and they looked in all the corners. They sought and sought everywhere.

At last the bear looked into the hopper and saw the trembling boy. He dragged him out and tore him to pieces.

༄

16

Wirreenun the Rainmaker

(Australian)

The country was stricken with a drought. The rivers were all dry except the deepest holes in them. The grass was dead, and even the trees were dying. The bark dardurr of the blacks were all fallen to the ground and lay there rotting, so long was it since they had been used, for only in wet weather did the blacks use the bark dardurr; at other times they used only whatdooral, or bough shades.

The young men of the Noongahburrah murmured among themselves, at first secretly, at last openly, saying: 'Did not our fathers always say that the Wirreenun could make, as we wanted it, the rain to fall? Yet look at our country—the grass blown away, no doonburr seed to grind, the kangaroo are dying, and the emu, the duck, and the swan have flown to far countries. We shall have no food soon; then shall we die, and the Noongahburrah be no more seen on the Narrin. Then why, if he is able, does not Wirreenun inake rain?'

Soon these murmurs reached the ears of the old Wirreenun. He said nothing, but the young fellows noticed that for two or three days in succession he went to the waterhole in the creek and placed in it a willgoo willgoo—a long stick, ornamented at the top with white cockatoo feathers—and beside the stick he placed two big gubberah, that is, two big, clear pebbles which at other times he always secreted about him, in the folds of his waywah, or in the band or net on his head. Especially was he careful to hide these stones from the women.

At the end of the third day Wirreenun said to the young men: 'Go you, take your comeboos and cut bark sufficient to make dardurr for all the tribe.'

The young men did as they were bade. When they had the bark cut and brought in Wirreenun said: 'Go you now and raise with ant-bed a high place, and put thereon logs and wood for a fire, build the ant-bed about a foot from the ground. Then put you a floor of ant-bed a foot high whereever you are going to build a dardurr.'

And they did what he told them. When the dardurr were finished, having high floors of ant-bed and water-tight roofs of bark, Wirreenun commanded the whole camp to come with him to the waterhole; men, women, and children; all were to come. They all followed him down to the creek, to the waterhole where he had placed the willgoo willgoo and gubberah. Wirreenun jumped into the water and bade the tribe follow him, which they did. There in the water they all splashed and played about. After a little time Wirreenun went up first behind one black fellow and then behind another, until at length he had been round them all, and taken from the back of each one's head lumps of charcoal. When he went up to each he appeared to suck the back or top of their heads, and to draw out lumps of charcoal, which, as he sucked them out, he spat into the water. When he had gone the round of all, he went out of the water. But just as he got out a young man caught him up in his arms and threw him back into the water. This happened several times, until Wirreenun was shivering. That was the signal for all to leave the creek. Wirreenun sent all the young people into a big bough shed, and bade them all go to sleep. He and two old men and two old women stayed outside. They loaded themselves with all their belongings piled up on their backs, dayoorl stones and all, as if ready for a flitting. These old people walked impatiently around the bough shed as if waiting a signal to start somewhere. Soon a big black cloud appeared on the horizon, first a single cloud, which, however, was soon followed by others rising all round. They rose quickly until they all met just overhead, forming a big black mass of clouds. As soon as this big, heavy, rainladen looking cloud was stationary overhead, the old people went into the bough shed and bade the young people wake up and come out and look at the sky. When they were all roused Wirreenun told them to lose no time, but to gather together all their possessions and hasten to gain the shelter of the bark dardurr. Scarcely were they all in the dardurrs and their spears well hidden when there sounded a terrific clap of thunder, which was quickly followed by a regular cannonade, lightning flashes shooting across the sky, followed by instantaneous claps of deafening thunder. A sudden flash of lightning, which lit a pathway, from heaven to earth, was followed by such a terrific clash that the blacks thought their very camps were struck. But it was a tree a little distance off. The blacks huddled together in their dardurrs, frightened to move, the children crying with fear, and the dogs crouching towards their owners.

'We shall be killed,' shrieked the women. The men said nothing but looked as frightened.

Only Wirreenun was fearless. 'I will go out,' he said, 'and stop the storm from hurting us. The lightning shall come no nearer.'

So out in front of the dardurrs strode Wirreenun, and naked he stood there facing the storm, singing aloud, as the thunder roared and the lightning flashed, the chant which was to keep it away from the camp:

'Gurreemooray, mooray,

Durreemooray, mooray, mooray,' &c.

Soon came a lull in the cannonade, a slight breeze stirred the trees for a few moments, then an oppressive silence, and then the rain in real earnest began, and settled down to a steady downpour, which lasted for some days.

When the old people had been patrolling the bough shed as the clouds rose overhead, Wirreenun had gone to the waterhole and taken out the willgoo willgoo and the stones, for he saw by the cloud that their work was done.

When the rain was over and the country all green again, the blacks had a great corrobboree and sang of the skill of Wirreenun, rainmaker to the Noongahburrah.

Wirreenun sat calm and heedless of their praise, as he had been of their murmurs. But he determined to show them that his powers were great, so he summoned the rainmaker of a neighbouring tribe, and after some consultation with him, he ordered the tribes to go to the Googoorewon, which was then a dry plain, with the solemn, gaunt trees all round it, which had once been black fellows.

When they were all camped round the edges of this plain, Wirreenun and his fellow rainmaker made a great rain to fall just over the plain and fill it with water.

When the plain was changed into a lake, Wirreenun said to the young men of his tribe: 'Now take your nets and fish.'

'What good?' said they. 'The lake is filled from the rain, not the flood water of rivers, filled but yesterday, how then shall there be fish?'

'Go,' said Wirreenun. 'Go as I bid you; fish. If your nets catch nothing then shall Wirreenun speak no more to the men of his tribe, he will seek only honey and yams with the women.'

More to please the man who had changed their country from a desert to a hunter's paradise, they did as he bade them, took their nets and went into the lake. And the first time they drew their nets, they were heavy with goodoo, murree, tucki, and bunmillah. And so many did they catch that all the tribes, and their dogs, had plenty.

Then the elders of the camp said now that there was plenty everywhere, they would have a borah that the boys should be made young men. On one of the ridges away from the camp, that the women should not know, would they prepare a ground.

And so was the big borah of the Googoorewon held, the borah which was famous as following on the triumph of Wirreenun the rainmaker.

17

The Story of Sayen

(Filipino)

In the depths of a dark forest where people seldom went, lived a wizened old Alan. The skin on her wrinkled face was as tough as a carabao hide, and her long arms with fingers pointing back from the wrist were horrible to look at. Now this frightful creature had a son whose name was Sayen, and he was as handsome as his mother was ugly. He was a brave man, also, and often went far away alone to fight.

On these journeys Sayen sometimes met beautiful girls, and though he wanted to marry, he could not decide upon one. Hearing that one Danepan was more beautiful than any other, he determined to go and ask her to be his wife.

Now Danepan was very shy, and when she heard that Sayen was coming to her house she hid behind the door and sent her servant, Laey, out to meet him. And so it happened that Sayen, not seeing Danepan, married Laey, thinking that she was her beautiful mistress. He took her away to a house he had built at the edge of the forest, for though he wished to be near his old home, he dared not allow his bride to set eyes on his ugly mother.

For some time they lived happily together here, and then one day when Sayen was making a plow under his house, he heard Laey singing softly to their baby in the room above, and this is what she sang:

'Sayen thinks I am Danepan, but Laey I am. Sayen thinks I am Danepan, but Laey I am.'

When Sayen heard this he knew that he had been deceived, and he pondered long what he should do.

The next morning he went to the field to plow, for it was near the rice-planting time. Before he left the house he called to his wife:

'When the sun is straight above, you and the baby bring food to me, for I shall be busy in the field.'

Before he began to plow, however, he cut the bamboo supports of the bridge which led to the field, so that when Laey and the baby came with his food, they had no sooner stepped on the bridge than it went down with them and they were drowned. Sayen was again free. He took his spear and his shield and head-ax and went at once to the town of Danepan, and there he began killing the people on all sides.

Terror spread through the town. No one could stop his terrible work of destruction until Danepan came down out of her house, and begged him to spare part of the people that she might have some from whom to borrow fire. Her great beauty amazed him and he ceased killing, and asked her to prepare some betel-nut for him to chew, as he was very tired. She did so, and when he had chewed the nut he spat on the people he had killed and they came to life again. Then he married Danepan and took her to his home.

Now it happened about this time that the people of Magosang were in great trouble. At the end of a successful hunt, while they were dividing the meat among themselves, the Komow, a murderous spirit that looks like a man, would come to them and ask how many they had caught. If they answered, 'Two', then he would say that he had caught two also; and when they went home, they would find two people in the town dead. As often as they went to hunt the Komow did this, and many of the people of Magosang were dead and those living were in great fear. Finally they heard of the brave man, Sayen, and they begged him to help them. Sayen listened to all they told, and then said:

'I will go with you to hunt, and while you are dividing the meat, I will hide behind the trees. When the Komow comes to ask how many deer you have, he will smell me, but you must say that you do not know where I am.'

So the people went to hunt, and when they had killed two deer, they singed them over a fire and began to divide them. Just then the Komow arrived and said:

'How many have you?'

'We have two,' replied the people.

'I have two also,' said the Komow, 'but I smell Sayen.'

'We do not know where Sayen is,' answered the people; and just then he sprang out and killed the Komow, and the people were greatly relieved.

Now when Kaboniyan, a great spirit, heard what Sayen had done, he went to him and said:

'Sayen you are a brave man because you have killed the Komow. Tomorrow I will fight with you. You must remain on the low ground by the river, and I will go to the hill above.'

So the following day Sayen went to the low ground by the river. He had not waited long before he heard a great sound like a storm, and he knew that Kaboniyan was coming. He looked up, and there stood the great warrior, poising his spear which was as large as a big tree.

'Are you brave, Sayen?' called he in a voice like thunder as he threw the weapon.

'Yes,' answered Sayen, and he caught the spear.

This surprised Kaboniyan, and he threw his head-ax which was as large as the roof of a house, and Sayen caught that also. Then Kaboniyan saw that this was indeed a brave man, and he went down to Sayen and they fought face to face until both were tired, but neither could overcome the other.

When Kaboniyan saw that in Sayen he had found one as strong and brave even as himself, he proposed that they go together to fight the people of different towns. And they started out at once. Many people were killed by this strong pair, and why they themselves could never be captured was a great mystery. For it was not known that one was the spirit Kaboniyan, and the other the son of an Alan.

If he was surrounded in a river, Sayen would become a fish and hide so that people could not find him. And if he was entrapped in a town, he would become a chicken and go under the house in a chicken-coop. In this way he escaped many times.

Finally one night after he had killed many in one town, the people decided to watch him, and they saw him go to roost with the chickens. The next day they placed a fish trap under the house near the chicken-coop, and that night when Sayen went under the house he was caught in the trap and killed.

18

How the Tiger Got His Stripes

(Brazilian)

Once upon a time, ages and ages ago, so long ago that the tiger had no stripes upon his back and the rabbit still had his tail, there was a tiger who had a farm. The farm was very much overgrown with underbrush and the owner sought a workman to clear the ground for him to plant.

The tiger called all the beasts together and said to them when they had assembled, 'I need a good workman at once to clear my farm of the underbrush. To the one of you who will do this work I offer an ox in payment.'

The monkey was the first one to step forward and apply for the position. The tiger tried him for a little while but he was not a good workman at all. He did not work steadily enough to accomplish anything. The tiger discharged him very soon and he did not pay him.

Then the tiger hired the goat to do the work. The goat worked faithfully enough but he did not have the brains to do the work well. He would clear a little of the farm in one place and then he would go away and work on another part of it. He never finished anything neatly. The tiger discharged him very soon without paying him.

Next the tiger tried the armadillo. The armadillo was very strong and he did the work well. The trouble with him was that he had such an appetite. There were a great many ants about the place and the armadillo could never pass by a sweet tender juicy ant without stopping to eat it. It was lunch time all day long with him. The tiger discharged him and sent him away without paying him anything.

At last the rabbit applied for the position. The tiger laughed at him and said, 'Why, little rabbit, you are too small to do the work. The monkey, the goat, and the armadillo have all failed to give satisfaction. Of course a little beast like you will fail too.'

However, there were no other beasts who applied for the position so the tiger sent for the rabbit and told him that he would try him for a little while.

The rabbit worked faithfully and well, and soon he had cleared a large portion of the ground. The next day he worked just as well. The tiger thought that he had been very lucky to hire the rabbit. He got tired staying around to watch the rabbit work. The rabbit seemed to know just how to do the work anyway, without orders, so the tiger decided to go away on a hunting trip. He left his son to watch the rabbit.

After the tiger had gone away the rabbit said to the tiger's son, 'The ox which your father is going to give me is marked with a white spot on his left ear and another on his right side, isn't he?'

'O, no,' replied the tiger's son. 'He is red all over with just a tiny white spot on his right ear.'

The rabbit worked for a while longer and then he said, 'The ox which your father is going to give me is kept by the river, isn't he?'

'Yes,' replied the tiger's son.

The rabbit had made a plan to go and get the ox without waiting to finish his work. Just as he started off he saw the tiger returning. The tiger noticed that the rabbit had not worked so well when he was away. After that he stayed and watched the rabbit until the whole farm was cleared. Then the tiger gave the rabbit the ox as he had promised.

'You must kill this ox,' he said to the rabbit, 'in a place where there are neither flies nor mosquitoes.'

The rabbit went away with the ox. After he had gone for some distance he thought he would kill him. He heard a cock, however, crowing in the distance and he knew that there must be a farm yard near. There would be flies of course. He went on farther and again he thought that he would kill the ox. The ground looked moist and damp and so did the leaves on the bushes. Since the rabbit thought there would be mosquitoes there he decided not to kill the ox. He went on and on and finally he came to a high place where there was a strong breeze blowing. 'There are no mosquitoes here,' he said to himself. 'The place is so far removed from any habitation that there are no flies, either.' He decided to kill the ox.

Just as he was ready to eat the ox, along came the tiger. 'O, rabbit, you have been such a good friend of mine,' said the tiger, 'and now I am so very, very hungry that all my ribs show, as you yourself can see. Will you not be a good kind rabbit and give me a piece of your ox?'

The rabbit gave the tiger a piece of the ox. The tiger devoured it in the twinkling of an eye. Then he leaned back and said, 'Is that all you are going to give me to eat?'

The tiger looked so big and savage that the rabbit did not

dare refuse to give him any more of the ox. The tiger ate and ate and ate until he had devoured that entire ox. The rabbit had been able to get only a tiny morsel of it. He was very, very angry at the tiger.

One day not long after the rabbit went to a place not far from the tiger's house and began cutting down big staves of wood. The tiger soon happened along and asked him what he was doing.

'I'm getting ready to build a stockade around myself,' replied the rabbit. 'Haven't you heard the orders?' The tiger said that he hadn't heard any orders.

'That is very strange,' said the rabbit. 'The order has gone forth that every beast shall fortify himself by building a stockade around himself. All the beasts are doing it.'

The tiger became very much alarmed. 'O, dear! O, dear! What shall I do,' he cried. 'I don't know how to build a stockade. I never could do it in the world. O, good rabbit! O, kind rabbit! You are such, a very good friend of mine. Couldn't you, as a great favour, because of our long friendship, build a stockade about me before you build one around yourself?'

The rabbit replied that he could not think of risking his own life by building the tiger's fortifications first. Finally, however, he consented to do it.

The rabbit cut down great quantities of long sharp sticks. He set them firmly in the ground about the tiger. He fastened others securely over the top until the tiger was completely shut in by strong bars. Then he went away and left the tiger.

The tiger waited and waited for something to happen to show him the need of the fortifications. Nothing at all happened.

He got very hungry and thirsty. After a while the monkey passed that way.

The tiger called out, 'O, monkey, has the danger passed?'

The monkey did not know what danger the tiger meant, but he replied, 'Yes.'

Then the tiger said, 'O, monkey, O, good, kind monkey, will you not please be so kind as to help me out of my stockade?'

'Let the one who got you in there help you out,' replied the monkey and he went on his way.

Along came the goat and the tiger called out, 'O, goat, has the danger passed?'

The goat did not know anything about any danger, but he replied, 'Yes.'

Then the tiger said, 'O, goat, O, good kind goat, please be so kind as to help me out of my stockade.'

'Let the one who got you in there help you out,' replied the goat as he went on his way.

Along came the armadillo and the tiger called out, 'O, armadillo, has the danger passed?'

The armadillo had not heard of any danger, but he replied that it had passed.

Then the tiger said, 'O, armadillo, O, good, kind armadillo, you have always been such a good friend and neighbour. Please help me now to get out of my stockade.'

'Let the one who got you in there help you out,' replied the armadillo as he went on his way.

The tiger jumped and jumped with all his force at the top of the stockade, but he could not break through. He jumped and jumped with all his might at the front side of the stockade, but he could not break through. He thought that never in the world would he be able to break out. He rested for a little while and as he rested he thought. He thought how bright the sun was shining outside. He thought what good hunting there was in the jungle. He thought how cool the water was at the spring. Once more he jumped and jumped with all his might at the back side of the stockade. At last he broke through. He did not get through, however, without getting bad cuts on both his sides from the sharp edges of the staves. Until this day the tiger has stripes on both his sides.

19

The King and the Apple

(Georgian)

There was and there was not at all (of God's best may it be!), there was a king. When the day of his death was drawing nigh, he called his son to him, and said: 'In the day when thou goest to hunt in the east, take this coffer, but only open it when thou art in dire distress.'

The king died, and was buried in the manner he had wished. The prince fell into a state of grief, and would not go outside the door. At last the ministers of state came to the new king, and proposed to him that he should go out hunting. The king was delighted with the idea, and set out for the chase with his suite.

They went eastwards, and killed a great quantity of game. On their way home, the young monarch saw a tower near the road, and wished to know what was in it. He asked one of his viziers to go and try to find out about it. He obeyed, but first said:

'I hope to return in three days, and if I do not I shall be dead.'

Three days passed, and the vizier did not return. The king sent a second, a third, a fourth, but not one of them came back. Then he rose and went himself. When he arrived, he saw written over the door: 'Enter and thou wilt repent; enter not and thou wilt repent.'

'I must do one or the other,' said the king to himself, 'so I shall go in.'

He opened the door and went in. Behold! There stood twelve men with drawn swords. They took his hand and led him into twelve rooms. When he was come into the twelfth, he saw a golden couch, on which was stretched a boy of eight or nine years of age. His eyes were closed, and he did not utter a word. The king was told:

'Thou mayst ask him three questions, but if he does not understand and answer all of them, thou must lose thy head.'

The king became very sad, but at last remembered the coffer his father had given him. 'What greater misfortune can I have than to lose my head?' said he to himself. He took out the coffer and opened it; from it there fell out an apple, which rolled towards the couch. 'What help can this be to me?' said the king.

But the apple began to speak, and told the following tale to the boy: 'A certain man was travelling with his wife and brother, when night fell, and they had no food. The woman's brother-in-law went into a neighbouring village to buy bread; on the way he met brigands, who robbed him and cut off his head. When his brother did not return, the man went to look for him; he met the same fate. The next day the unhappy woman went to seek them, and there she saw her husband and brother-in-law lying in one place with their heads cut off; around was a pool of blood. The woman sat down, tore her hair, and began to weep bitterly. At that moment there jumped out a little mouse. It began to lick the blood, but the woman took a stone, threw it at the mouse, and killed it. Then the mouse's mother came out and said: 'Look at me, I can bring my child back to life, but what canst thou do for thy husband and his brother?' She pulled up an herb, applied it to the little mouse, and it was restored to life. Then they both disappeared in their hole. The woman rejoiced greatly when she saw this; she also plucked of the same herb, put the heads on the bodies, and applied it to them. Her husband and brother-in-law both came back to life, but alas! She had put the wrong heads on the bodies. Now, my sage youth! Tell me, which was the woman's husband?' concluded the apple.

He opened his eyes, and said: 'Certainly it was he who had the right head.'

The king was very glad.

'A joiner, a tailor, and a priest were travelling together at one time,' began the apple. 'Night came on when they were in a wood; they lighted a huge fire, had their supper, and then said: "Do not let us be deprived of employment, each of us shall in turn watch, and do something in his trade." The joiner's turn came first. He cut down a tree, and out of it he fashioned a man. Then he lay down, and went to sleep, while the tailor mounted guard. When he saw the wooden man, he took off his clothes and put them on it. Last of all, the priest acted as sentinel. When he saw the man he said: "I will pray to God that He may give this man a soul." He prayed, and his wish was granted.'

'Now, my boy, canst thou tell me who made the man?'

'He who gave him the soul.'

The king was pleased, and said to himself: 'That is two.' The apple again went on: 'There were a diviner, a physician, and a swift runner. The diviner said: "There is a certain prince who is ill with such and such a disease." The physician said: "I know a cure for it." "I will run with it," said the swift runner. The physician prepared the medicine, and the man ran with it. Now tell me who cured the king's son?' said the apple.

'He who made the medicine,' replied the boy. When he had given the three answers, the apple rolled back into the casket, and the king put it in his pocket. The boy arose, embraced the king, and kissed him: 'Many men have been here, but I have not been able to speak before: now tell me what thou wishest, and I will do it.' The king asked that his viziers might be restored to life, and they all went away with rich presents.

20

The Fairy Bonze

(Chinese)

In a certain well-known and populous city in one of the north-western provinces of China, there once resided a man of the name of Meng. Everyone knew about him. His fame had spread not only throughout the town, but also far away into the country beyond; for of all the merchants who carried on business in this great commercial centre he was the wealthiest and the most enterprising.

He had begun life as a poor lad; but through great strength of purpose and positive genius for business, he had steadily risen step by step, until by the time our story opens, he had become exceedingly wealthy and was the acknowledged leader in all the great undertakings for which the city was famous.

Meng had always gained the admiration and affection of every one who became acquainted with him. He was of an artless, open-hearted disposition which won men to him, and his reputation for generosity made his name fragrant throughout the entire region in which he lived.

Forty years ago he had come to the city in search of employment. His father was a farmer in one of the outlying country districts; but Meng, discontented with the dullness of the life and with the strain and trouble brought upon his home by bad seasons, started out for the great town to make his fortune.

All that he possessed he carried on his person. His stock-in-trade consisted simply of a stout bamboo pole and a good strong rope, the usual signs of a porter; but his willingness to oblige, and the hearty, pleasant way in which he performed his arduous duties, gained him the goodwill of all who employed him. Before many months had passed he was in constant demand, and was slowly saving up money that was to enable him to rise from the position of a coolie and to enter some business which would give him a more honourable place in society.

He had a shrewd and common-sense mind which enabled him to take advantage of any trade-opening that presented itself, and as he had a genial and happy disposition, everyone who had had any business relations with him was glad to do all in his power to give him a lift in the upward road along which he had made up his mind to travel. The result was that before many years had passed away he had established himself in a very lucrative line of business which brought a steady flow of wealth into his coffers.

In time he opened branches in distant cities, and his fame reached the far-off provinces in the East, where the merchant-princes who had dealings with him counted him as one of the most trustworthy of their clients, to whom they were glad to give as much credit as he might desire.

There was one delightful feature about Meng, and that was the intense sympathy he had for his fellow-creatures. He had a heart of gold that no prosperity could spoil; no one who ever applied to him for relief was sent away empty-handed.

The struggling shopkeeper made his humble appeal when fate seemed determined to crush him, and the substantial loan that Meng made to him without hesitation kept him from closing his shutters and once more set him on his feet to commence the struggle again. The widow who had been left in absolute poverty had but to state her case, when with a countenance beaming with compassion and with eyes moist at her piteous story, Meng would make such arrangements for her and her children that the terror of starvation was lifted from her heart, and she left his presence with a smiling face and with heart-felt words of praise for the man who by his generosity had given her a new glimpse of life.

The character of Meng's mind may well be discovered from the manner in which he distributed a considerable portion of his riches amongst those who had been born under an unlucky star, and upon whom an unhappy fate had pressed heavily in the distribution of this world's goods and favours.

The generous men in China are not the rich. It is true that occasionally one does hear of a munificent donation having been made by some millionaire, but the public is never deceived by these unusual outbursts of generosity. There is a selfish motive at the back of nearly every one of them, for the hope of the donors is that by gaining the favour of the mandarins they may obtain some high official position which will enable them to recoup themselves most handsomely for any sums they may have expended in charity.

Meng's deeds, however, were always purely unselfish, and no idea of reward ever entered his head. He was moved solely by a sincere desire to alleviate human suffering. The look of gladness that flashed over the faces of those whom he assisted, their gleaming eyes, and the words of gratitude that burst from their lips, were to him the sweetest payment that could possibly be made to him in return for the sums he had given away.

That Meng's fame had travelled far was shown by an occurrence which was destined to have a considerable influence on the fortunes of his only son, Chin, in whom his whole soul was bound up.

One day he received a letter from the head of a most aristocratic family in a distant city, begging that he would consent to an alliance with him. This man wrote that he had a daughter, who was declared by all who saw her to be possessed of no ordinary beauty, and he wished to have her betrothed to Meng's son. Meng's reputation for goodness and for love to his fellow-men had reached his ears, and he was anxious that their families should be united by the marriage of two young people.

The rich merchant, whose heart always retained its childlike spirit, was delighted with this proposal, which had come to him spontaneously, and not through the intrigues of a middle-woman. He was also touched by the apparently generous spirit of the writer, so he at once responded to the appeal. After some little correspondence, the betrothal was drawn up in due form, and the young couple were bound to each other by legal ties which no court in the Empire would ever dream of unloosing.

Just at this juncture, when the tide in Meng's affairs seemed at its highest, there appeared at his doors one day a venerable-looking bonze, who asked to be received as a guest for a few days, as he was on a pilgrimage to a famous shrine and was tired out with the long journey that he had already made.

Meng, who was a very devout and religious man, gave the old priest a most hearty welcome. He placed one of the best rooms in the house at his disposal, and treated him with all the generous hospitality which he was accustomed to bestow upon men of his profession, who in travelling from one monastery to another had very often stayed with him for a night or two before proceeding further on their way.

Now, this priest had such pleasing manners, and was so refined and cultivated, that he completely captured the hearts of all the household, so much so that Meng insisted upon his prolonging his stay. The result was that months went by and the bonze still remained with him as his guest.

Everyone in the house seemed to be attracted by this stranger, so winning were his ways, and so full of quiet power were his whole bearing and character. He was affable and pleasant with all, but he seemed to take most pleasure in the company of Chin, over whom he soon came to exercise a very powerful influence.

Their habit was to wander about on the hillside, when the priest would entertain his young friend with stories of the wonderful things he had seen and the striking adventures he had met with. His whole aim, however, seemed to be not so much to amuse Chin as to elevate his mind with lofty and noble sentiments, which were instilled into him on every possible occasion.

It was also their custom to retire every morning to some outhouses at the extremity of the large garden attached to the dwelling-house, where undisturbed they could converse together upon the many questions upon which the bonze was ready to discourse. One thing, however, struck Chin as very singular, and this was that the bonze made him collect certain curiously-shaped tiles, and bury them in the earthen floors of these little-used buildings. Chin would have rebelled against what he considered a child-like proceeding, but he was restrained by the profound love and veneration he felt for his companion.

At length the day came when the bonze announced that he must proceed upon his journey. He had already, he declared, stayed much longer than he had originally intended, and now the imperative call of duty made it necessary that he should not linger in the house where he had been so royally treated.

Seeing that he was determined in his purpose, Meng wanted to press upon him a considerable sum of money to provide for any expenses to which he might be put in the future. This, however, the bonze absolutely refused to accept, declaring that his wants were few, and that he would have no difficulty in meeting them by the donations he would receive from the different temples he might pass on his way to his destination.

Little did Meng dream that the guest from whom he was parting with so heavy a heart was a fairy in disguise. Yet such was the case. The rulers of the far-off Western Heaven, who had been greatly moved by Meng's noble and generous life in succouring the distressed and the forlorn, had sent the bonze to make arrangements to meet a certain calamitous crisis which was soon to take place in the home of the wealthy merchant.

A few months after the good bonze had left them, a series of disasters fell with crushing effect upon the house of Meng. Several firms which owed him very large sums of money suddenly failed, and he found himself in such financial difficulties that it was utterly impossible for him to pay his debts.

In consequence, Meng was utterly ruined, and after paying out all that he possessed, even to the uttermost cash, found himself absolutely penniless. This so wrought upon his mind that he became seriously ill, and after a few days of intense agony, his spirit vanished into the Land of Shadows, and his wife and son were left desolate and bereaved.

After a time Chin bethought himself of the wealthy and distinguished man who had been so anxious to recognize him as a son-in-law, and after consultation with his mother, who was completely broken-hearted, he set off for the distant city in which his proposed father-in-law lived. Chin hoped that the latter's heart would be moved by the disasters which had befallen his father, and that he would be willing to extend him a helping hand in his hour of dire sorrow, when even Heaven itself seemed to have abandoned him and to have heaped upon his head calamities such as do not often occur to the vilest of men.

Weary and worn with the long journey, which he had been compelled to make on foot, he arrived one day about noon at the gates which led into the spacious courtyard of the palatial mansion in which his father-in-law lived. The doors, however, were shut and barred, as though some enemy was expected to storm them and carry off the property within.

Chin called loudly to the porter to open them for him, but to his amazement he was told that orders had been received from the master of the house that he was not to be admitted on any terms whatsoever.

'But are you aware who I am?' he asked. 'Do you not know that the man who owns this building is my father-in-law, and that his daughter is my promised wife? It ill becomes you therefore to keep me standing here, when I should be received with all the honours that a son-in-law can claim.'

'But I have been specially warned against you,' replied the surly gatekeeper. 'You talk of being a son-in-law, but you are greatly mistaken if you imagine that any such kinship is going to be recognized in this house. News has reached my master of the utter failure of your father's business, and of his death, and he declares that he does not wish to be mixed up in any way with doubtful characters or with men who have become bankrupt.'

Chin, who was imbued with the fine and generous spirit of his father, was so horrified at these words that he fled from the gate, determined to suffer any indignity rather than accept a favour from a man of such an ignoble disposition as his father-in-law apparently possessed.

He was crossing the road with his heart completely cast down, and in absolute despair as to how he was ever to get back to his home again, when a woman in one of the low cottages by the roadside, beckoned him to come in and sit down.

'You seem to be in distress, sir,' she said, 'and to be worn out with fatigue, as though you had just finished a long journey. My children and I are just about to sit down to our midday meal, and we shall be so pleased if you will come and partake of it with us. I have just been watching you as you stood at the gate of that wealthy man's house, and I saw how roughly you were treated. Never mind,' she continued, 'Heaven knows how you have been wronged, and in time you will be avenged for all the injury you have suffered.'

Comforted and gladdened by these kindly words and by the motherly reception given him by this poor woman, Chin started out on his return journey, and after much suffering finally reached his home. Here he found his mother in the direst poverty, and with a heart still full of the deepest woe because of the death of her noble-minded husband.

Almost immediately after Chin had been refused admission to the house of his father-in-law, the latter's daughter, Water-Lily, became aware of the insulting way in which he had been treated. She was grieved beyond measure, and with tears in her eyes and her voice full of sorrow, she besought her mother to appeal to her father on her behalf, and to induce him to give up his purpose of arranging a marriage for her with a wealthy man in the neighbourhood.

'My father may plan another husband for me,' she said, 'but I shall never consent to be married to anyone but Chin. All the rites and ceremonies have been gone through which bind me to him as long as I live, and to cast him off now because calamity has fallen upon his home is but to invite the vengeance of the Gods, who will surely visit us with some great sorrow if we endeavour to act in a way contrary to their laws.'

The piteous appeals of Water-Lily had no effect upon her father, who hurried on the arrangements for his daughter's wedding to the new suitor, anxious to marry her off in order to prevent the unfortunate Chin from appearing again to claim her as his wife.

She, however, was just as determined as her father, and when she realized that all her entreaties and prayers had produced not the slightest effect upon him, and that in the course of a few days the crimson bridal chair would appear at the door to carry her away to the home of her new husband, she determined to adopt heroic methods to prevent the accomplishment of such a tragedy.

Next morning, as dawn began to break, the side-gate of the rich man's house was stealthily opened, and a degraded-looking beggar-woman stepped out into the dull grey streets, and proceeded rapidly towards the open country beyond.

She was as miserable a specimen of the whining, cringing beggar as could have been met with in any of the beggar-camps where these unhappy outcasts of society live. She was dressed in rags which seemed to be held together only by some invisible force. Her hair was tied up in disjointed knots, and looked as if no comb had ever tried to bring it into order. Her face was black with grime, and a large, dirty patch was plastered over one of her ears in such a way that its shape was completely hidden from the gaze of those who took the trouble to cast a passing glance upon her.

Altogether she was a most unattractive object; and yet she was the most lovely woman in all that region, for she was none other than Water-Lily, the acknowledged beauty of the town, who had adopted this disguise in order to escape from the fate which her father had planned for her.

For several weary months she travelled on, suffering the greatest hardships, and passing through adventures, which, if some gifted writer had collected them into a volume, would have thrilled many a reader with admiration for this brave young maiden. Though reared and nurtured in a home where every luxury was supplied her, yet she endured the degradation and privations of a beggar's life rather than be forced to be untrue to the man whom she believed Heaven had given her as a mate.

One evening, as the shadows were falling thickly on the outer courtyard of the desolate house where Chin lived, a pitiful-looking beggar-woman stood timidly at the front door, gazing with wistful looks into the room which faced the street. Not a sound did she utter, not a single word escaped her lips to indicate that she had come there to obtain charity.

In a few minutes Chin's mother came out from a room beyond. When she saw this ragged, forlorn creature standing silently as though she were afraid that some word of scorn and reproach would be hurled at her, she was filled with a great and overmastering pity, and stepping up to her she began to comfort her in loving, gentle language.

To her astonishment this draggled, uncleanly object became violently affected by the tender, motherly way in which she was addressed. Great tear-drops trickled down her grimy face, leaving a narrow, snow-like line in their wake. Presently she was convulsed with sobs that shook her whole body, whilst she wrung her hands as though some great sorrow was gripping her heart.

Mrs Meng was deeply affected by the sight of this unhappy woman, and whilst she was gazing at her with a look of profound sympathy, the broad patch which had concealed and at the same time disfigured the beggar's countenance, suddenly dropped to the ground.

The effect of this was most startling, for a pair of as beautiful black eyes as ever danced in a woman's head were now revealed to Mrs Meng's astonished gaze. Looking at the stranger more intently, she saw that her features were exquisitely perfect, and had the grace and the poetry which the great painters of China have attributed to the celebrated beauties of the Empire.

'Tell me who you are,' she cried, as she laid her hand tenderly and affectionately on her shoulder, 'for that you are a common beggar-woman I can never believe. You must be the daughter of some great house, and have come here in this disguise in order to escape some great evil.

'Confide in me,' she continued, 'and everything that one woman can do for another, I am willing to do for you. But come in, dear child, and let us talk together and devise some plan by which I can really help you, for I feel my heart drawn towards you in a way I have never felt for any stranger before.'

Mrs Meng then led her into her bedroom, where Water-Lily threw off the outer garments in which she had appeared to the public as a beggar, and telling her wonderful story to Chin's mother, she revealed herself as her daughter-in-law.

But though her romantic arrival into this gloomy and distressed home brought with it a sudden gleam of happiness, the great question as to how they were to live had still to be solved. They were absolutely without means, and they could only hope to meet their meagre expenses by the sale of the house in which they were living.

At last this plan was discussed, and it was decided that the unused buildings, in which Chin and the Buddhist priest had been accustomed to spend a part of every day together, should be first of all disposed of.

In order to have some idea as to how much these outhouses were worth, Chin went to see what condition they were in, so that he might fix a price for them. As they had not been used for some time, the grass had grown rank about them, and they had a dilapidated and forlorn air which made Chin fear that their market value would not be very great.

Entering in by an open door, which a creeping vine, with the luxuriance of nature, was trying to block up, Chin looked round with a feeling of disappointment sending a chill into his very heart.

The air of the place was damp and musty. The white mould could be seen gleaming on the walls, as if it wished to give a little colour to the sombre surroundings. Great cobwebs flung their streaming banners from the beams and rafters overhead, whilst smaller ones, with delicate lace-like tracery, tried to beautify the corners of the windows, through which the light from the outside world struggled to enter the gloomy room.

Throwing the windows wide open to let in as much sunshine as was possible, Chin soon became convinced that the market value of this particular part of his property would be very small, and that unless he carried out extensive repairs, it would be impossible to induce any one to entertain the idea of buying it.

While he was musing over the problem that lay before him, his eye caught a silvery gleam from a part of the earthen floor, where the surface had evidently been scratched away by some animal that had wandered in.

Looking down intently at the white, shining thing which had caught his attention, Chin perceived that it was one of the tiles that the bonze had made him bury in the earth, and when he picked it up, he discovered to his amazement that in some mysterious manner it had been transformed into silver! Digging further into the earth, he found that the same process had taken place with every tile that had been hidden away beneath the floor of this old and apparently useless building.

After some days occupied in transporting his treasure to a safe place in his dwelling-house, Chin realized by a rough calculation that he was now the possessor of several millions' worth of dollars, and that from being one of the poorest men in the town he had become a millionaire with enormous wealth at his command.

Thus did the Gods show their appreciation of the noble life of Mr Meng, and of his loving sympathy for the poor and the distressed, by raising his fallen house to a higher pinnacle of prosperity than it had ever attained even during his lifetime.

21

The Strong Man and the Dwarf

(Gurian)

There came from far-off lands a strong man who had nowhere met his match, and challenged any one in the whole kingdom to wrestle with him. The king gathered his folk together, but, to his wonder, could not for a long time find anybody ready to face the strong man, till, at last, there stood forth a weak insignificant-looking dwarf, who offered to wrestle with the giant.

Haughtily looking down on his adversary, the giant carelessly turned away, thinking that he was befooled. But the dwarf asked that his strength should be put to the proof before the struggle began.

The giant angrily seized a stone, and, clasping it in his fingers, squeezed moisture out of it.

The dwarf cunningly replaced the stone by a sponge of the same appearance, and squeezed still more moisture out of it.

The giant then took another stone, and threw it so violently on the ground that it became dust.

The dwarf took a stone, hid it under the ground, and threw on the ground a handful of flour, to the great astonishment of the giant.

Stretching forth his hand to the dwarf, the giant said: 'I never expected to find so much strength in such a small man, I will not wrestle with you; but give me your hand in token of friendship and brotherhood.'

After this, the giant asked the dwarf to go home with him. But first he asked the dwarf why he had not pressed his hand in a brotherly manner. The dwarf replied that he was unable to moderate the force of his pressure, and that more than one man had already died from the fearful force of his hand. The new brothers then set out together. On their way to the giant's house, they came to a stream which had to be forded.

The dwarf, fearing to be carried away by the current, told the strong man that he was suffering from belly-ache, and did not therefore wish to go into the cold water, so he asked to be carried over.

In the midst of the stream, the strong man, with the dwarf on his shoulders, suddenly stopped and said: 'I have heard that strong people are heavy, but I do not feel you on my shoulders. Tell me how this is, for God's sake.'

'Since we have become brothers,' replied the dwarf, 'I have no right to press with all my weight upon you, and did I not support myself by holding on to the sky with one hand, you could never carry me.'

But the strong man, wishing to test his strength, asked the dwarf to drop his hand for a moment, whereupon the dwarf took from his pocket two nails, and stuck the sharp points of them in the shoulders of the strong man.

The giant could not endure the pain, and begged the dwarf to lighten his burden at once, i.e. to lay hold of heaven with one hand again.

When they had reached the other side, the two new friends soon came to the strong man's house. The giant, wishing to give a dinner to the dwarf, proposed that they should share the work of getting it ready, that one of them should take the bread out of the oven, while the other went to the cellar for wine.

The dwarf saw in the oven an immense loaf which he could never have lifted, so he chose to go to the cellar for wine. But when he had descended, he was unable even to lift the weights on the top of the jars, so, thinking that by this time the giant would have taken the loaf out of the oven, he cried: 'Shall I bring up all the jars?'

The giant, alarmed lest the dwarf should spoil his whole year's stock of wine, by digging the jars out of the ground, where they were buried, rushed down into the cellar, and the dwarf went upstairs.

But great was the astonishment of the dwarf when he found that the bread was still in the oven, and that he must take it out, willy-nilly. He succeeded with difficulty in dragging a loaf to the edge of the oven, but then he fell with the hot bread on top of him, and, being unable to free himself, was almost smothered.

Just then the giant came in, and asked what had happened. The dwarf replied: 'As I told you this morning, I am suffering from a stomach-ache, and, in order to soothe the pain, I applied the hot loaf as a plaster.' ... Then the giant came up, and said: 'Poor fellow! How do you feel now, after your plaster?' 'Better, thank God,' replied the dwarf, 'I feel so much better that you can take off the loaf.' ... The giant lifted the loaf, and the two then sat down to dinner. Suddenly the giant sneezed so hard that the dwarf was blown up to the roof, and seized a beam, so that he should not fall down again. The giant looked up with astonishment, and asked: 'What does this mean?' The dwarf angrily replied: 'If you do such a vulgar thing again I shall pull this beam out and break it over your stupid head.' The giant made humble excuses, and promised that he would never sneeze again during dinner time; he then brought a ladder by which the dwarf came down....

22

The Enchanted Princesses

(Czech)

In the days of King Bambita, his two noble daughters oppressed the people, laying heavy taxes on them without the king's knowledge. The people cursed them, and the curses did their work. The princesses vanished. The king sent some of his servants to look for the princesses. But the servants came back empty-handed. None of them had been able to find the princesses.

Now, a captain and a lieutenant heard of the king's trouble. So the lieutenant went to the king, and 'I see,' says he, 'that you are in trouble. I will go and look for the princesses.'

'How much do you want for it?' asked the king.

'Twenty pounds.'

The king agreed, and gave him the money. 'If you find them,' said he, 'half of my kingdom is yours.'

The lieutenant and the captain had plenty of money now, so they went to an inn and passed the time drinking. On the third day the captain said: 'To-day I will go to the king. If he gave you twenty pounds, he is certain to give me more.'

So he went to the king and said: 'I see that your majesty is in trouble. I should like to go and look for the princesses.'

'How much do you want for it?' said the king.

'Thirty pounds.'

Well, the king gave him the money without any more ado, adding that, if he found the princesses, he would get half of his kingdom.

They fell to drinking again and had a splendid time.

There was a drummer near them, and he heard them saying that they were to look for the princesses. So he went to the king and said: 'I hear that your majesty is prostrated by sore trouble. I, too, would like to look for the princesses.'

'How much do you want for it?'

'Forty pounds, at least.'

The king gave him the money without more ado. The two officers and the drummer left that inn for another, and so they went on spending their money recklessly in one drinking-house after another. The drummer went with the other two, but he was more careful than they were. He was not such a spendthrift as the two officers.

They asked him where he meant to go.

'Wherever you go, I will go too,' he replied.

'Then why don't you join us and lead a gay life?'

'That I can't do until I know where to find the princesses.'

They invited him to join them, but he refused to do it.

At last they bought some bread and other food, and they all set out together on their journey. They came to a dark forest, and for a fortnight they searched it through and through, but they could find nothing. They couldn't find their way out of the forest either, so they agreed that one of them should climb to the top of the highest tree to see which way they ought to go. The drummer, being the youngest, climbed up a pine-tree. He called out:

'I can see a cottage. Look, I will throw my hat towards it, and do you follow the hat.'

Well, they went on until they reached the cottage.

'Go into the room,' says the drummer.

'After you,' said both the officers at once.

So the drummer stepped inside, and an old crone welcomed him.

'Welcome, Drummer Anthony,' said she. 'How did you get here?'

'I have come to deliver the princesses, and only for that.'

'Well, you will find them, but those other two fellows will get them from you by a trick.'

She gave him a rope three hundred fathoms long and told him to bind it round his body. She also gave him some wine and a sponge. Then she said: 'Not far from here there is a well. When you come to it, you must say that you will let yourself down into the well, if the other fellows will drink the fountain dry.'

When they got to the well, the captain and the lieutenant began to drink the fountain, but it was just as full as before.

'If we kept on drinking this fountain till doomsday,' they said, 'we could not drink it dry.'

So the drummer took the sponge, and at once the water began to disappear, and soon the well was dry. They began to quarrel as to who should go down the well. The one on the right side said the other ought to go, but at last they agreed that the drummer, who was the lightest, should go.

So he went down, and, when he reached the bottom of the well, he found a stone there. He drew it aside, and then he saw the light of the other world. He lowered himself on the rope into the other world. There he saw a beautiful palace. He went towards it. When he reached it, he saw that the table was laid for two persons. He ate his meal and then went into the second room. There he laid himself down to sleep, and when he awoke in the morning, he found the Princess Anne in the third room.

'Welcome,' she said; 'what has brought you here?'

He told her that he had come to deliver her.

She said: 'I don't know whether you will succeed in that. Here is a sword; see if you can brandish it.'

The drummer took hold of the sword, but he could not even lift it, it was so heavy.

Then the princess gave him a ring. 'Take this,' she said, 'and whenever you think of me, you will become strong. I have to hold the dragon in my lap for a whole hour. As soon as he comes, he will smell a man. But you must cut him in two, for then I shall be delivered. Just at nine o'clock he comes.'

Just at nine o'clock the palace began to tremble and the dragon came in. But the drummer encountered him and struck him in two with the sword.

After that the princess took him into another room. 'Now you have delivered me,' she said. 'But my sister is in worse trouble still. She has to hold a dragon in her lap for two hours, and that dragon is even stronger than this one.'

Then they went into the fourth room, where was the Princess Antonia. She, too, greeted him, and told him that he would be able to deliver her if he could brandish the sword beside her. He tried, but he could not even move it. Then she gave him a ring and told him that, whenever he thought of her, he would have the strength of two hundred men. She said, too, that if he succeeded in setting her free she would marry him.

Soon eleven o'clock came. The hall began to tremble and the dragon appeared. But, as he was coming in, Anthony was ready for him near the door, and he managed to cut the dragon in two.

Now, when the two princesses had been set free, they gathered all the precious stones they could to take with them, and went to the opening that led into the world. But the drummer had quite forgotten the old crone's warning about the other two fellows, and he sent the princesses up before him. Each of the officers took a princess for himself, and the drummer was left behind at the bottom of the well. When his turn came, he was careful enough to tie a stone to the rope. His companions on the top pulled it up a little way and then suddenly let it drop, throwing down other stones into the well to kill the drummer. But he had remembered the crone's warning that his friends would try to trick him. So he jumped aside and remained there in the other world.

He went back to the palace and entered the seventh room. On the table were three boxes. He opened the first and found a whistle inside it. He blew the whistle, and in came some generals and asked what was his majesty's will. He said he had only whistled to find out if they were attending to their duty. Then he looked into the second box, and there he saw a bugle. He blew the bugle, and in came some officers, who said just what the generals had said. In the third box he found a drum. He beat the drum, and immediately he was surrounded by infantry and cavalry, a great multitude of soldiers. He asked whether any of them had ever been in Europe. Two men were found among them who had been shipwrecked.

'Where is the ship?' said the drummer.

'Here on the seacoast,' they replied.

At that, Anthony decked himself out in a royal robe and started on his travels for Europe.

Meanwhile the two princesses had reached home. One was engaged to be married to the lieutenant, the other to the captain. But when the time for the wedding came, both the princesses, still thinking of Anthony, asked for a delay of one year, and their royal father granted their request.

Anthony arrived safely in that land. He met a traveller and said to him, 'Look here, why should you not change clothes with me?'

He was glad to do so, and Anthony went on to the town in which the princesses lived and sought out a goldsmith. He asked the goldsmith for work.

'I haven't work enough for myself,' said the goldsmith.

'Well,' said the drummer, 'I have had an order for two rings, although I was only walking the street.'

'You are a lucky fellow,' said the goldsmith, and his wife, when she heard of it, spoke in the drummer's favour, so he was taken on as assistant.

'Now,' said he, 'give me what I want and I will make the rings. But nobody must enter my room: I will take my meals in at the door.'

On the third day one ring was finished, and this one was meant for the Princess Anne.

'You must take this ring to the Princess Anne, master,' said he.

'So I will,' said the goldsmith; 'but what is your price for it?'

'A thousand pounds,' said he.

'If that's so, I won't go. They would put me in jail.'

'Be easy,' said Anthony, 'nothing will happen to you.'

So the goldsmith went to the palace, and sent in a message that his assistant had made a ring for the Princess Anne. She sent a message that she had not ordered a ring, but she would look at it. As soon as she saw it, she asked: 'How much do you want for this?' He replied that he was almost afraid to say that it was worth a thousand pounds.

'Oh! It is worth much more than that,' she said, and she paid the sum at once.

The goldsmith returned home and told his wife what he had got for the ring. She wondered what sort of person their new assistant was. The master brought the money to him, but the assistant would not accept it.

'You can keep the money for yourself,' he said, 'and I have just finished the ring for the Princess Antonia. You will have to go to the palace again with this.'

This time the master-goldsmith was ready enough to go. 'How much am I to ask for this ring?' he said.

'Ask two thousand pounds.'

So he was brought to the princess, and he told her that his apprentice had made a ring for her. She answered that she had not ordered a ring. 'However, show it to me.'

As soon as she glanced at it, she said: 'How much do you want for this?'

'Two thousand pounds.'

'Oh! It's worth much more than that,' she said.

So she paid down the money and told the master-goldsmith to fetch his assistant to her. As soon as the master came home, he told his wife everything. She was still more astonished.

'O Lord!' she said, 'I cannot understand it at all.'

The master told Anthony that the princess bade him come and see her.

'She can come to me,' was his reply.

When the princess heard that, she lost no time, but took some royal garments for him, and drove to Anthony's house in the royal coach. She went straight to him and said, 'I am come to bring you home with me, Anthony.'

She bade him put on the royal robe she had brought with her for him, and they drove together to the palace, and their marriage was celebrated not long after.

The two officers thought the king would banish them or inflict some punishment upon them, but he pardoned them and gave them sufficient money to live at the court. Anthony himself did not care for royalty. He and his wife arranged that they would return to the place where he had first found the princesses. So they departed for that land, but a storm drove them on shore near to the place where he had met the old crone. She gave him welcome.

'So you are back again,' she said.

They explained to her that what they wished was to go back to that palace beneath the fountain.

'Well,' she said, 'I will show you the way to the other world, and I will let you down the well.'

They came to the opening, and Anthony was about to enter the well, but the old hag begged him to wait with her and let the princess go on before.

So the princess was let down to the bottom of the well, and then the crone said: 'I won't let you follow her unless you first cut off my head.'

'This is a strange way to repay the good you have done me,' said Anthony.

'Well, unless you promise this you will never see your princess again.'

So he had to promise, and with that she waved her wand and a road appeared, which led them straight to the princess. Then Anthony struck off the crone's head, and they found themselves amid crowds of farmers who were ploughing and soldiers standing at attention, and one and all welcoming their new lords. For this land was an enchanted land, and the old crone was a witch.

23

Danílo the Unfortunate

(Russian)

Good Prince Vladímir had many henchmen and serfs in the city of Kíev, and amongst them there was Danílo the Unfortunate, the noble. And on Sundays Prince Vladímir used to give all his servants goblets filled with wine, but Danílo good hard blows; and on great feast days every one was sated, but Danílo had nothing.

On the eve of Easter Sunday Prince Vladímir summoned Danílo the Unfortunate, and he gave him eighty score of sable skins, and he bade him sew a *shúba* (fur mantle) for the feast: the sable skins were not prepared, and the buttons had not been moulded, and the buttonholes had not been made. In the buttons he was bidden mould the wild beasts of the wood and to sew into the buttonholes all the seabirds.

Danílo the Unfortunate loathed the task, so he hurled it away, and he went outside. He went out on his road and way, and shed tears. An old woman came to meet him. 'Look, Danílo,' she said, 'do not rend yourself asunder: why are you crying, Danílo the Unfortunate?'

'Oh, you old fatty!' he exclaimed, 'shivers and shakes, quivers and quakes! Be off! This has nothing to do with you!' Then he went on a little way and thought, 'Why did I bid her remove?' So he approached her again and said, '*Bábushka*, little dove, forgive me: this is my trouble. Prince Vladímir has given me eighty score of sable skins, of which I am to make a shúba in the morning. If only the buttons had been moulded and the silken buttonholes sewn! But there are to be lions moulded on to the buttons, and there are to be shepherds embroidered on to the buttonholes that should have sung and warbled. How am I to set about it? It would be better for me to drink *vódka* behind the counter.'

Then the old woman, with her patched skirt, said, 'Oh, I am now "Bábushka" and your "little dove"! Do you go to the border of the blue sea, and stand in front of the grey oak: at the hour of midnight the blue sea will boil over and Chúdo-Yúda, the Old Man of the Sea, will come out to you: he has no hands, no feet, and he has a grey beard. Take hold of him by his beard and beat him until he asks you, "Why do you beat me, Danílo the Unfortunate?" Then you are to answer, "I am beating you for this reason: let me see the Swan, the fair maiden; let her body glint through her wings, and through her body let her bones appear, and from bone to bone let the marrow run like a flowing string of pearls."'

Then Danílo the Unfortunate went to the blue sea, and he stood in front of the dusky oak: and at midnight the blue sea was disturbed and Chúdo-Yúda, the Old Man of the Sea, appeared before him. He had no hands, he had no feet, and his beard was grey. Danílo seized him by his beard and began to beat him on to the grey earth. Then at last Chúdo-Yúda asked him: 'Why do you beat me, Danílo the Unfortunate?' 'For this reason: let me see the Swan, the fair maiden; let her body glint through her wings, and through her body let her bones appear, and from bone to bone let the marrow run like a flowing string of pearls.'

Very soon the Swan, the fair maiden, swam up to the shore, and she spoke in this wise:

'Is it work on your way,
Or for sloth do you stay?'

'Oh, Swan, fair maiden, I have a double task: Prince Vladímir has bidden me sew a shúba, and the sables are not prepared, the buttons are not moulded, and the buttonholes are not sewn.'

'You take me with you, and it will all be done in time.'

Then he began to think in his thoughts, 'How shall I take her with me?'

'Now, Danílo, what are you thinking?'

'I must do as you say: I will take you with me.'

So she flapped her wings, and she moved her little head, and said, 'Turn to me with your white face; we will build for ourselves a princely house. Shake your locks, that our house may have rooms.' Then twelve youths appeared, all of them carpenters, sawyers, stone-hewers; and they set to work, and the house was soon ready.

Then Danílo took her by her right hand, and he kissed her on her sweet lips, and he led her into the princely home. They sat down at a table, ate and drank. They refreshed themselves, and their hands met at one table. 'Now, Danílo, go to rest and to bed; think of nothing else; it will all be done.' So she laid him to sleep and herself went out to the crystal flight of steps. And she waved her pinions and she shook her little head: 'My father,' she cried, 'send me your craftsmen!'

And the twelve youths appeared and asked, 'Swan-bird, fair maiden, what do you bid us do?'

'Sew me this shúba at once: the sables are not prepared, the buttons are not moulded, the buttonholes are not sewn.'

So they set to work: one of them made the sables ready and sewed the shúba, one of them worked the forge and moulded the buttons, and one of them sewed the buttonholes, and in a minute, wondrously, the shúba was made.

Then the Swan-bird, the fair maiden, came up and woke Danílo the Unfortunate: 'Arise, my dear friend, the shúba is ready, and the church-bells are ringing in the city of Kíev: it is time for you to arise and to prepare for matins.'

Danílo arose, put on the shúba, and went: she looked out of the window, stayed, gave him a silver staff, and bade him, 'When you leave matins, stand on the right side of the choir as the choir leave, raise your hands and strike the sable shúba, and the birds will sing joyously and the lions roar fearsomely. Then take the shúba from your shoulders and array Prince Vladímir at that instant, lest he forget us. He will then summon you as a guest, and will give you a glass of wine. Do not drink the glass to the bottom: if you drink it to the bottom no good will befall you; and do not boast of me: do not boast that we built a house together in a single night.'

Danílo took the silver staff and hied away, and she again stayed him on his course, and she gave him three little eggs, two of silver, one of gold, and said, 'With the silver eggs give the Easter greeting to the Prince and the Princess, but the golden one keep and live your life along with it.'

Danílo the Unfortunate bade farewell to her and went to matins. All the people wondered. 'Look what a fine man Danílo the Unfortunate has become: he has made the shúba and he has brought it with him for the feast.'

After the Mass, he went up to the Prince and Princess, and he gave them the Easter greeting, but carelessly took out the golden egg. Alyósha Popóvich saw this, the Mocker of Women. As they went out of the church, Danílo the Unfortunate struck himself on the breast with the silver staff, and the birds sang and the lions roared; and all the folk were amazed and gazed at Danílo. But Alyósha Popóvich, the Mocker of Women, dressed himself as a sorry beggar and asked for holy alms. They all gave to him; only Danílo the Unfortunate alone said and thought, 'What shall I give him? I have nothing to give.' So, as it was Easter Day, he gave him the golden egg. Alyósha Popóvich took that golden egg and changed into his former garb.

Prince Vladímir summoned them all to him, all to his palace to dessert: so they ate and drank and were refreshed, and they exalted themselves. Danílo drank until he was drunk; and, when he was drunk, made boast of his wife. Alyósha Popóvich bragged at the feast that he knew Danílo's wife. But Danílo said, 'If you know my wife you may cut off my head; and, if you do not know her, you shall forfeit your own.'

So Alyósha Popóvich, the Mocker of Women, went whither his eyes might go, and he went and wept.

Then the old woman met him on his way and asked, 'Why are you weeping, Alyósha Popóvich?'

'Go away, old woman with the swollen belly; I have naught to do with you.'

'Yet I shall be of service to you.'

Then he began to ask her, 'O my own grandmother, what did you wish to tell me?'

'Ha! Am I now your own grandmother?'

'O, I was boasting I knew Danílo's wife!'

'O *bátyushka*, how do you know her: was there any little bird that told you? Do you go up to a certain house and invite her to feast with the Prince. She will wash herself, busk herself, and put a little chain out of the window. You take that chain and show it to Danílo the Unfortunate.'

So Alyósha Popóvich, the Mocker of Women, went to the window jamb, and called the Swan-bird, the fair maiden, to dine with the Prince. She was starting to wash herself, busk herself, and make ready for the feast, and that moment Alyósha Popóvich seized her little chain, ran up into the palace, and showed it to Danílo the Unfortunate.

So Prince Vladímir said to Danílo the Unfortunate, 'I see now that you must forfeit your head.'

'Let me go home and bid farewell to my wife.' So he went home and said, 'O fair Swan-maiden, what have I done? I became drunk and I bragged of you and have lost my life.'

'I know it all, Danílo the Unfortunate. Go, summon the Prince and Princess here as your guests, and all the burghers and generals and field-marshals and *boyárs*.'

'But the Prince will not come out in the mud and the mire!' (For the roads were bad, and the blue sea became stormy; the marshes surged and opened.)

'You are to tell him: "Have no fear, Prince Vladímir: across the rivers have been built hazel-tree bridges, the transoms are of oak covered with cloth of purple and with nails of tin. The shoes of the doughty warrior will not be soiled, nor will the hoofs of his horse be smeared."'

So Danílo the Unfortunate invited them as guests; and the

Swan-bird, the fair maiden, stepped out to her window, flapped her wings, shook her little head, and there was a bridge laid from her house to the palace of Prince Vladímir. It was covered with cloth of purple, tacked in with tacks of tin; and on one side flowers grew, nightingales sang, and on the other side apple trees and fruits bloomed and ripened.

The Prince and Princess made ready to be guests, and they set out on their journey with all their noble host with them, crossed the first river, which ran with splendid beer. And very many soldiers fell down by that beer. Then they advanced to the second river, which ran with wonderful mead, and more than half of the brave host bent down to drink the mead and rolled on their sides. So they came to the third river, which ran with glorious wine. Here all the officers bent down and drank till they were drunk. At the fourth river powerful *vódka* flowed. And the Prince looked backwards: all of his generals were lying on their backs. Only the Prince was left with three companions—with the Princess, Alyósha Popóvich, the Mocker of Women, and Danílo the Unfortunate.

Then the invited guests arrived, and they entered into the lofty palace: there were tables standing, and the table-cloths were of silk, and the chairs painted with many colours. They sat down at the tables: there were all sorts of dishes and of foreign drinks. There were no bottles, no mere pints—entire rivers flowed! Prince Vladímir and the Princess drank nothing, tasted nothing, only looked on. When would the Swan, the fair maiden, come out? And they sat long at the table, waited for her long, until it was time to go home. Danílo the Unfortunate called her once, and twice, and a third time, but she would not come and see her guests.

Alyósha Popóvich, the Mocker of Women, then said, 'If this had been my wife I should have taught her to obey!'

Then the Swan-bird, the fair maiden, came out and stood at the window, and she said these words: 'This is how we teach our husbands!' And so she flapped her wings, moved her little head, and flew about: and there the guests sat on mounds in the bog.

One way the waters tossed,
On the other lay woe,
On the third side naught but moss,
On the fourth side—Oh!

'Get up, Prince, and avaunt! Let Danílo sit at the head of the table.'

So they went back all the way to their palace, and they were covered with mud from head to foot.

24

The Twin Brothers

(Czech)

Once there was a princess, and she was under a curse and enchantment, so that she had to spend her life in the shape of a fish. One day a woman happened to be working in the meadow by the river, and she saw a flock of birds flying above the river and talking to the fish. The woman wondered what it was that was there, so she went to the waterside and looked in. All she saw was a fish swimming about. So she said: 'I should like to eat you, fish. I feel sure you would do me good.'

Now, when she said that, the fish answered: 'You could save me. You will have twin sons, although you have never had any children before.'

The woman said that, if she could help her in that, there was nothing the fish could ask that she would not do to deliver her.

The fish answered: 'Catch me and take me to your field. There you must bury me and plant a rose-tree over me. When the roses first come into bloom you will bear twin sons. After three years, dig in the place where you buried me and you will find two swords, and these you must keep. Your mare will have two foals and your bitch will have two pups, and each of your twins will have a sword, a horse, and a dog.

Those swords will have the virtue that they will help your sons to victory over everybody. I shall be delivered as soon as my body has rotted.'

When the twin sons grew up they were very clever, and so they said: 'We must try our luck in the world. We are bold enough. One of us will go to the East and one to the West. Each of us must look at his sword every morning to see if the other needs his help. For the sword will begin to rust as soon as one of us is in peril.'

So they cast lots which way they should go, and each of them took his sword, his horse, and his dog, and away they went.

The first rode through deep forests, and he met a fierce dragon and a lion; so he attacked the dragon, which had nine heads. The lion stayed quiet while the knight attacked the dragon, and at last he succeeded in cutting one of the dragon's heads off. He felt tired then, and the lion took his place; then the knight cut two more heads off the dragon. And so it went on till he had all the heads cut off. Then he cut out the tongues from all the nine heads and kept them, and so went forward on his adventurous journey.

Now, it chanced that there were some woodcutters in these forests, and one of them collected all the dragon's heads, having come across them by chance. That dragon used to come to the town and devour one person every visit. This time the lot had fallen upon the princess, and so she was to be devoured by the dragon. So the town was all hung with black cloth. The woodcutter knew all about this, so he went with the heads to the town to sue for the princess, for it had been proclaimed that whoever killed the dragon should be her husband. When the princess saw that such a low-born man was to be her husband she was taken aback, and tried by all the means in her power to delay the wedding.

The knight happened to come to the town just then, and he saw a good inn, so he rode up to it. The innkeeper came at once to ask what he could do for him. Now, there were other guests there, and it was a busy place. The guests were all talking of the one matter: when the princess was going to marry the man who had killed the dragon. The wedding ought to have been long ago, but the bride and her parents kept putting it off. The knight listened to all this talk, and then he asked:

'Are you sure that it was that woodcutter who killed the dragon?'

They answered that it certainly was, for the heads were preserved in the palace.

The knight said nothing, but when he thought the proper time had come he rode to the palace. The princess saw him from the window, and she wondered who it might be. He was ushered in, and he went straight to the princess and told her everything. He asked her whether he might attend the wedding.

She answered: 'I am not at all pleased with my marriage. I would much rather marry you, sir.'

He asked her why.

'If he killed the dragon he must be a great man.'

'He is such a low-born man,' said she, 'that it is not likely that he killed the dragon.'

'I should like to see him,' said he.

So they brought the woodcutter before him, and the knight asked to see the heads. So they brought the heads. He looked at the heads and said:

'There are no tongues in these heads. Where are the tongues?'

Then he turned to the woodcutter: 'Did you really kill the cruel dragon?' he said.

The woodcutter persisted in his story.

'And how did you cut the heads off?'

'With my hatchet.'

'Why, you couldn't do it with your hatchet. You are a liar.'

The woodcutter was taken aback and did not know what to say. He was frightened already, but he said: 'It happened that the dragon didn't have any tongues.'

The knight produced the tongues and said: 'Here are the tongues, and it was I who killed the cruel dragon.'

The princess took hold of him and embraced and kissed him, and she was ready to marry him on the spot. As for the woodcutter, he was kicked out in disgrace, and they put him into jail for some time too. So the princess married the knight and they lived happily together.

One day, looking out of the window, he saw in the distance, among the mountains, a black castle. He asked his wife what castle it was and to whom it belonged.

'That is an enchanted castle, and nobody who goes into it ever returns.'

But he could not rest, and he was eager to explore the castle. So one morning he ordered his horse to be saddled, and, accompanied by his dog, he rode to the castle. When they reached it they found the gate open. As he went in he saw men and animals all turned to stone. In the hall an old hag was sitting by the fire. When she saw him she pretended to tremble.

'Dear lord,' said she, 'bind your dog. He might bite me.'

He said: 'Do not be afraid. He will do you no harm.'

He bent down to pat the dog, and at that moment the hag took her wand and struck him with it. He was turned to stone, and his horse and dog too.

The princess waited for her lord, but he did not return. She mourned for him, and the citizens, who loved their lord, were grieved at his loss.

Now, the other brother looked at his sword, and the sword began to rust; so he was sure that his brother was in trouble. He felt that he must help him, so he rode off in that direction and came to the town. The town was hung with black flags. As he rode through the streets the citizens saw him, and they thought he was their lord, for he had a horse and a dog just like their lord's horse and dog. When the princess saw him, she embraced him and said: 'Where have you been so long, my dear husband?'

He said that he had lost his way in the forest and that he had fallen among robbers, and, since he had no choice, he had to pretend to be a robber too, and to promise to stay with them and to show them good hiding-places. The robbers, so he said, admitted him to be of their company, and he had not been able to escape before this.

Everybody was delighted, and the lord's brother was careful enough not to say that he was only the brother. But, whenever they went to bed, he put his sword between himself and the lady. The princess was troubled at this, and she tried to find different explanations for the conduct of her supposed husband. One morning, as he was looking out of the window, he saw that same castle, and he asked what castle it was.

She answered: 'I have told you already that it is an enchanted castle, and that nobody who goes there ever returns.'

So he thought: 'It is surely there that my brother is.'

He ordered his horse to be saddled and, without saying a word to anybody, he rode off to the castle. As soon as he entered the castle he saw his brother and his dog turned to stone. He saw, too, all the petrified knights and their horses, and the hag sitting and keeping up the fire.

He said: 'You old hag, unless you bring my brother to life again I'll hew you in pieces with this sword of mine.'

The hag knew that the sword had magical virtues, and so she said:

'Pray, sir, do not be angry with me. Take that box there and rub the ointment beneath his nose and he will come to life again.'

'Curse you, you evil old hag; do it yourself, and instantly.'

And he went and caught hold of her wand and struck her with it, and at once she was turned into stone. He had not meant to do that, for he did not know that the wand had such power. He took the box and rubbed the ointment beneath his brother's nose, and the brother came to life again. Then he anointed all the others who had been turned to stone, and they all came to life again. As for the hag, he left her there just as she was.

Then the brothers rode off to the princess. When she saw them, she did not know which of them was her husband, they were so like one another.

So she said: 'What am I to do now? Which of you is my lord?'

They came before her and bade her choose the right one. But still she hesitated. So her husband went up to her and took her by the hand and said: 'I am the right one and that is my brother.'

He told her everything, and she was glad that her real husband had come again. So they lived happily together, and, as for the other brother, he went to seek his fortune elsewhere.

25

The Fox and the King's Son

(Georgian)

There was once a king who had a son. Every one treated him badly, and chased him away. Even passers-by looked upon him with disfavour. The prince thought and thought, and at last he mounted his horse, took his bow and arrow, and departed from his father's palace.

When he had gone some distance he came into a sheltered wood. He wandered about until he found a suitable nook. He built for himself a mud hut, and dwelt there.

Every day the prince went out to hunt. He would shoot a stag or a roebuck, and bring it home. After he had eaten as much as he wanted, there was always enough meat left for the next day, but he never ate it the next day, as he went hunting again, and there was thus always a quantity of food left over.

A fox perceived this, and every day, when the prince had gone out to the chase, he stole into the hut and ate all the food that was left; then he stole away again. Some time passed thus. Then the fox said: 'There is no bravery in this! I carry away all his meat secretly, yet there is plenty. I will show myself to him.'

Once when the prince was hunting, the fox stole in, and, when his hunger was satisfied, he went about arranging everything. When the prince came home, the fox leaped out in front of him. The prince drew his bow, and was just about to shoot him, when the fox cried out: 'Do not kill me, and I will help to make thy fortune!' The prince did not kill him, and the fox attended to the horse, and led it about, until the sweat dried off its coat. They lived thus for some time. The fox lighted the fire, tidied the hut, and did all the work.

But, in spite of this, there was still meat left. 'I will go and find some one who will help to eat it,' said the fox. He went out, and saw a wolf hardly able to walk from want of food. It could scarcely move from the spot where it was. The fox said: 'Come home with me, and thou shalt have plenty of everything.' The wolf followed him. They both went into the hut, where the fox told his companion: 'I will tidy the house, thou must stay here, and when the master comes in attend to his horse.'

The master came, and on the saddle of his horse was slung a stag. The wolf sprang out to attend to the horse; the youth drew his bow, and was about to shoot the wolf, when the fox cried out: 'Do not kill him, he is a friend!' The prince did not kill him, but jumped down from his horse, took the stag, and went in. The wolf attended to the horse, and led him up and down, while the fox himself saw to the inside of the house; thus they lived for some time.

The fox noticed that there was much meat left even now. He ran out and brought in a famished bear. The wolf was sent for grass, the bear commanded to tend the horse, while the fox arranged the house. In a little time the prince came in, and when the bear jumped out to look after his horse he drew his bow to shoot him, but the fox cried out: 'Do not kill him, he is a friend!' The youth did not kill the bear, and he tended the horse and led it about; then the wolf came in with the grass, and gave it to the horse.

Some time passed. The fox saw that even yet there was meat to spare. He went out and sought until he found an eagle, which he brought home. He commanded the eagle to attend to the horse, sent the bear for grass, and the wolf for wood to burn, while he saw to household affairs. Thus each had his business to do. When the master returned, the eagle flew out to tend the horse. The prince was about to shoot him, when the fox cried out: 'Do not kill him, he is a friend!' The prince did not kill him, but thought to himself: 'What will this vile fox bring in next? I shall see all the game in the country here.' They lived thus some time.

Once the fox said to his master: 'Give us leave to go away for two weeks; at the end of that time we shall return to thee.' The master gave them leave, and thought to himself: 'I do not mind if I never see you again, for I am afraid of you all.' The fox, the wolf, the bear, and the eagle went away. They saw a glade in the wood, and rested there. The fox said to his companions: 'Now, let us build a good house for our master.' They all agreed, and set to work. The wolf cut down trees, the bear cut the wood into shape, and did the joiner work, the eagle carried it, and the fox gave orders. When the wood was ready, they set to and built the house. They built so beautiful a house that the prince could not have imagined one like it, even in his dreams. Everything was finished, but there was no furniture in it.

The fox arose and took his companions into a neighbouring town. They went into the bazaar, and looked at the house-furniture. Each one had his work to do again. The fox chose the goods, the wolf was ordered to break the shutters, the bear to carry the things to the door, and the eagle to take everything to the palace. They seized everything necessary for furnishing a house—domestic utensils, carpets and vessels. They carried them to the palace, and placed them there; so now all was finished, and there was nothing more left to wish for.

Two weeks had expired, so the four went home. The prince was hunting, but they went to meet him. They surrounded him, and would not let him pass. The fox cried out: 'I command thee to come with us whither we lead thee.' The prince was afraid, he did not know what it could mean, but went with them. In a little while they arrived in the glade. It was girt by a wall over which no bird could fly. They opened the gates and went inside. When the king's son saw, he was stupefied with surprise. Inside the wall was laid out a beautiful garden, with fountains playing, and there stood a magnificent palace. Then they said: 'We have made all this ready in two weeks, now live happily in it.' The prince rejoiced greatly, and gave hearty thanks to his fox.

Some time passed after this. The fox said: 'I must see if I can find a good wife for my master.' He came to the prince, and again asked a fortnight's absence. Then he went away and made a sledge. He harnessed the wolf and bear to it, and said to the eagle: 'Fly up high, and keep a watch; when thou seest a beautiful princess, seize her in thy claws and carry her off.' He himself sat down and acted as coachman. Thus they travelled from place to place.

In the villages, the fox played the trumpet, and the bear and the wolf leaped and danced along. Crowds of people came out to look. When they came to the capital, a maiden, fair as the sun, looked from her window, the eagle seized her in his claws, and flew off. The bear and the wolf turned round and started for home. When the people saw this, they all set off in pursuit. The fox was behind his companions, and the dogs came nearer, and almost touched his cloak, but in some way or other they all escaped, and brought the fair one to their master.

The king's son could scarcely stand on his feet for joy. The princess's father was in the greatest consternation, and said: 'To him who finds and brings back my daughter will I give the half of my kingdom.' But none was able to find trace of her. At last an old woman appeared, and said to the king: 'I will find thy daughter.' She arose and went forth. At last she came to the prince's house, and asked: 'Do ye not want an attendant? I will come for small wages.' The fox, wolf, bear, and even the beautiful princess herself, said: 'We do not want thee, we shall not take thee.' But the prince did not agree with them, and engaged her as servant.

The old woman served them faithfully for a long time, and did not harm them. Then one day, when the prince was asleep, the old woman wanted the princess to go out into the garden with her. She did not wish to go, but the old woman pressed her until she consented. When they came to the fountains, the old woman offered her some water. The princess refused it, but the old woman insisted. She placed a *litra* (large jar) full of water to her lips, and it suddenly swallowed up the princess. Then the old woman put it to her own mouth, and it swallowed her. The litra rolled away. The fox saw and pursued, but that which he sought was soon lost to sight.

The fox reproached his master, but it was no use saying anything now. He asked again for a fortnight's leave, made another sledge like the former, and harnessed the bear and wolf to it. He sat up on the seat, and held tambourines in his paws. He struck them, and the wolf and bear pranced and danced along. The eagle flew up high, and looked round. All the people in the land came out to gaze at the sight. The king was angry with his beautiful daughter, and said, 'Do not go out! Do not even look out.' The eagle watched for a long time, but could not see her. At last he caught a glimpse of the princess through a little window; he struck against it, broke it, seized the princess, and flew away. He rejoined his companions, and all hastened off.

They brought the princess to their master. The king collected all his army, and sent the old woman with it to the prince's palace. The fox saw them appearing in the distance like a swarm of flies. He ordered the eagle to carry stones up high in the air. When the army approached, the eagle let the stones fall on the men; the fox, the bear, and the wolf attacked them, and completely exterminated them. There escaped only one single man; they fell upon him too, gnawed one of his feet, and said: 'Go and tell thy king what has befallen his hosts.'

When the king saw his man, and heard the sad end of his army, he was out of his mind with grief. He assembled all the chief priests in his kingdom, went in front of them, and they all came on bended knees. When they were near, the fox saw them, and told his master. The prince ran out to meet them, raised them all on their feet, and took them into his house. The father and son-in-law became reconciled, and lived happily together. Then the fox said to his master: 'I am getting old now, and the day of my death will soon be here, promise to bury me in a fowl-house.' The prince promised. The fox said to himself: 'Come, I will see if my master means to keep his promise,' and he stretched himself out as if he were dead. When the prince saw the corpse, he ordered it to be taken away and thrown into the earth.

The fox was enraged, jumped up and cried out: 'Is this the way thou rememberest my goodness to thee? Well, since thou hast done thus, when I die you will all be cursed, and there will not remain a trace of you.' Some time after this the fox died. After his death, his word came to pass, and they were all destroyed. The wolf, the bear, and the eagle remained masters of the field.

26

The Mistaken Gifts

(Filipino)

When Siagon was about eight years old his parents began looking for a girl who would make a suitable wife. At last when they had decided on a beautiful maiden, who lived some distance from them, they sent a man to her parents to ask if they would like Siagon for a son-in-law.

Now when the man arrived at the girl's house the people were all sitting on the floor eating periwinkle, and as they sucked the meat out of the shell, they nodded their heads. The man, looking in at the door, saw them nod, and he thought they were nodding at him. So he did not tell them his errand, but returned quickly to the boy's parents and told them that all the people at the girl's house were favourable to the union.

Siagon's parents were very much pleased that their proposal had been so kindly received, and immediately prepared to go to the girl's house to arrange for the wedding.

Finally all was ready and they started for her house, carrying with them as presents for her parents two carabao, two horses, two cows, four iron kettles, sixteen jars of basi, two blankets, and two little pigs.

The surprise of the girl's people knew no bounds when they saw all this coming to their house, for they had not even thought of Siagon marrying their daughter.

27

The Eagle and the Whale

(Greenland, Eskimo)

In a certain village there lived many brothers. And they had two sisters, both of an age to marry, and often urged them to take husbands, but they would not. At last one of the men said:

'What sort of a husband do you want, then? An eagle, perhaps? Very well, an eagle you shall have.'

This he said to the one. And to the other he said:

'And you perhaps would like a whale? Well, a whale you shall have.'

And then suddenly a great eagle came in sight, and it swooped down on the young girl and flew off with her to a high ledge of rock. And a whale also came in sight, and carried off the other sister, carrying her likewise to a ledge of rock.

After that the eagle and the girl lived together on a ledge of rock far up a high steep cliff. The eagle flew out over the sea to hunt, and while he was away, his wife would busy herself plaiting sinews for a line wherewith to lower herself down the rock. And while she was busied with that work, the eagle would sometimes appear, with a walrus in one claw and a narwhal in the other.

One day she tried the line, with which she was to lower herself down; it was too short. And so she plaited more.

But as time went on, the brothers began to long for their sister. And they all set to work making crossbows.

And there was in that village a little homeless boy, who was so small that he had not strength to draw a bow, but must get one of the others to draw it for him every time he wanted to shoot. When they had made all things ready, they went out to the place where their sister was, and called to her from the foot of the cliff, telling her to lower herself down. And this she did. As soon as her husband had gone out hunting, she lowered herself down and reached her brothers.

Towards evening, the eagle appeared out at sea, with a walrus in each claw, and as he passed the house of his wife's brothers, he dropped one down to them. But when he came home, his wife was gone. Then he simply threw his catch away, and flew, gliding on widespread wings, down to where those brothers were. But whenever the eagle tried to fly down to the house, they shot at it with their bows. And as none of them could hit, the little homeless boy cried:

'Let me try too!'

And then one of the others had to bend his bow for him. But when he shot off his arrow, it struck. And when then the eagle came fluttering down to earth, the others shot so many arrows at it that it could not quite touch the ground.

Thus they killed their sister's husband, who was a mighty hunter.

But the other sister and the whale lived together likewise. And the whale was very fond of her, and would hardly let her out of his sight for a moment.

But the girl here likewise began to feel homesick, and she also began plaiting a line of sinew threads, and her brothers, who were likewise beginning to long for their sister, set about making a swift-sailing umiak. And when they had finished it, and got it into the water, they said:

'Now let us see how fast it can go.'

And then they got a guillemot which had its nest close by to fly beside them, while they tried to outdistance it by rowing. But when it flew past them, they cried:

'This will not do; the whale would overtake us at once. We must take this boat to pieces and build a new one.' And so they took that boat to pieces and built a new one.

Then they put it in the water again and once more let the bird fly a race with them. And now the two kept side by side all the way, but when they neared the land, the bird was left behind.

One day the girl said as usual to the whale: 'I must go outside a little.'

'Stay here,' said her husband, that great one.

'But I must go outside,' said the girl.

Now he had a string tied to her, and this he would pull when he wanted her to come in again. And hardly had she got outside when he began pulling at the string.

'I am only just outside the passage,' she cried. And then she tied the string by which she was held, to a stone, and ran away as fast as she could down hill, and the whale hauled at the stone, thinking it was his wife, and pulled it in. The brothers' house was just below the hillside where she was, and as soon as she came home, they fled away with her. But at the same moment, the whale came out from the passage way of its house, and rolled down into the sea. The umiak dashed off, but it seemed as if it were standing still, so swiftly did the whale overhaul it. And when the whale had nearly reached them, the brothers said to their sister:

'Throw out your hairband.'

And hardly had she thrown it out when the sea foamed up, and the whale stopped. Then it went on after them again, and when it came up just behind the boat, the brothers said: 'Throw out one of your mittens.'

And she threw it out, and the sea foamed up, and the whale pounced down on it. And then she threw out the inner lining of one of her mittens, and then her outer frock and then her inner coat, and now they were close to land, but the whale was almost upon them. Then the brothers cried:

'Throw out your breeches!'

And at the same moment the sea was lashed into foam, but the umiak had reached the land. And the whale tried to follow, but was cast up on the shore as a white and sun-bleached bone of a whale.

28

The Vengeance of the Goddess

(Chinese)

In a certain temple in the northern part of the Empire, there once lived a famous priest named Hien-Chung, whose reputation had spread far and wide, not merely for the sanctity of his life, but also for the supernatural powers which he was known to possess, and which he had exhibited on several remarkable occasions. Men would have marvelled less about him had they known that the man dressed in the long slate-coloured robe, with shaven head, and saintly-looking face, over which no one had ever seen a smile flicker, was in reality a pilgrim on his way to the Western Heaven, which he hoped to reach in time, and to become a fairy there.

One night Hien-Chung lay asleep in a room opening out of the main hall in which the great image of the Goddess of Mercy, with her benevolent, gracious face, sat enshrined amidst the darkness that lay thickly over the temple. All at once, there stood before him a most striking and stately-looking figure. The man had a royal look about him, as though he had been accustomed to rule. On his head there was a crown, and his dress was such as no mere subject would ever be allowed to wear.

Hien-Chung gazed at him in wonder, and was at first inclined to believe that he was some evil spirit who had assumed this clever disguise in order to deceive him. As this thought flashed through his mind, the man began to weep. It was pitiable indeed to see this kingly person affected with such oppressive grief that the tears streamed down his cheeks, and with the tenderness that was distinctive of him Hien-Chung expressed his deep sympathy for a sorrow so profound.

'Three years ago,' said his visitor, 'I was the ruler of this "Kingdom of the Black Flower." I was indeed the founder of my dynasty, for I carved my own fortune with my sword, and made this little state into a kingdom. For a long time I was very happy, and my people were most devoted in their allegiance to me. I little dreamed of the sorrows that were coming on me, and the disasters which awaited me in the near future.

'Five years ago my kingdom was visited with a very severe drought. The rains ceased to fall; the streams which used to fall down the mountain-sides and irrigate the plains dried up; and the wells lost the fountains which used to fill them with water. Everywhere the crops failed, and the green herbage on which the cattle browsed was slowly blasted by the burning rays of the sun.

'The common people suffered in their homes from want of food, and many of the very poorest actually died of starvation. This was a source of great sorrow to me, and every day my prayers went up to Heaven, that it would send down rain upon the dried-up land and so deliver my people from death. I knew that this calamity had fallen on my kingdom because of some wrong that I had done, and so my heart was torn with remorse.

'One day while my mind was full of anxiety, a man suddenly appeared at my palace and begged my ministers to be allowed to have an audience with me. He said that it was of the utmost importance that he should see me, for he had come to propose a plan for the deliverance of my country.

'I gave orders that he should instantly be brought into my presence, when I asked him if he had the power to cause the rain to descend upon the parched land.

'"Yes," he replied, "I have, and if you will step with me now to the front of your palace I will prove to you that I have the ability to do this, and even more."

'Striding out to a balcony which overlooked the capital, and from which one could catch a view of the hills in the distance, the stranger lifted up his right hand towards the heavens and uttered certain words which I was unable to understand.

'Instantly, and as if by magic, a subtle change crept through the atmosphere. The sky became darkened, and dense masses of clouds rolled up and blotted out the sun. The thunder began to mutter, and vivid flashes of lightning darted from one end of the heavens to the other, and before an hour had elapsed the rain was descending in torrents all over the land, and the great drought was at an end.

'My gratitude to this mysterious stranger for the great deliverance he had wrought for my kingdom was so great that there was no favour which I was not willing to bestow upon him. I gave him rooms in the palace, and treated him as though he were my equal. I had the truest and the tenderest affection for him, and he seemed to be equally devoted to me.

'One morning we were walking hand in hand in the royal gardens. The peach blossoms were just out, and we were enjoying their perfume and wandering up and down amongst the trees which sent forth such exquisite fragrance.

'As we sauntered on, we came by-and-by upon a well which was hidden from sight by a cluster of oleander trees. We stayed for a moment to peer down its depths and to catch a sight of the dark waters lying deep within it. Whilst I was gazing down, my friend gave me a sudden push and I was precipitated head first into the water at the bottom. The moment I disappeared, he took a broad slab of stone and completely covered the mouth of the well. Over it he spread a thick layer of earth, and in this he planted a banana root, which, under the influence of the magic powers he possessed, in the course of a few hours had developed into a full-grown tree. I have lain dead in the well now for three years, and during all that time no one has arisen to avenge my wrong or to bring me deliverance.'

'But have your ministers of State made no efforts during all these three years to discover their lost king?' asked Hien-Chung. 'And what about your wife and family? Have they tamely submitted to have you disappear without raising an outcry that would resound throughout the whole kingdom? It seems to me inexplicable that a king should vanish from his palace and that no hue and cry should be raised throughout the length and breadth of the land until the mystery should be solved and his cruel murder fully avenged.'

'It is here,' replied the spirit of the dead king, 'that my enemy has shown his greatest cunning. The reason why men never suspect that any treason has been committed is because by his enchantments he has transformed his own appearance so as to become the exact counterpart of myself. The man who called down the rain and saved my country from drought and famine has simply disappeared, so men think, and I the King still rule as of old in my kingdom. Not the slightest suspicion as to the true state of things has ever entered the brain of anyone in the nation, and so the usurper is absolutely safe in the position he occupies to-day.'

'But have you never appealed to Yam-lo, the ruler of the Land of Shadows?', asked Hien-Chung. 'He is the great redresser of the wrongs and crimes of earth, and now that you are a spirit and immediately within his jurisdiction, you should lay your complaint before him and pray him to avenge the sufferings you have been called upon to endure.'

'You do not understand,' the spirit hastily replied. 'The one who has wrought such ruin in my life is an evil spirit. He has nothing in common with men, but has been let loose from the region where evil spirits are confined to punish me for some wrong that I have committed in the past. He therefore knows the ways of the infernal regions, and is hand in glove with the rulers there, and even with Yam-lo himself. He is, moreover, on the most friendly terms with the tutelary God of my capital, and so no complaint of mine would ever be listened to for a moment by any of the powers who rule in the land of the dead.

'There is another very strong reason, too, why any appeal that I might make for justice would be disregarded. My soul has not yet been loosed from my body, but is still confined within it in the well. The courts of the Underworld would never recognize me, because I still belong to this life, over which they have no control.

'Only to-day,' he continued, 'a friendly spirit whispered in my ear that my confinement in the well was drawing to a close, and that the three years I had been adjudged to stay there would soon be up. He strongly advised me to apply to you, for you are endowed, he said, with powers superior to those possessed by my enemy, and if you are only pleased to exercise them I shall speedily be delivered from his evil influence.'

Now the Goddess of Mercy had sent Hien-Chung a number of familiar spirits to be a protection to him in time of need. Next morning, accordingly, he summoned the cleverest of these, whose name was Hing, in order to consult with him as to how the king might be delivered from the bondage in which he had been held for the three years.

'The first thing we have to do,' said Hing, 'is to get the heir to the Throne on our side. He has often been suspicious at certain things in the conduct of his supposed father, one of which is that for three years he has never been allowed to see his mother. All that is needed now is to get some tangible evidence to convince him that there is some mystery in the palace, and we shall gain him as our ally.

'I have been fortunate,' he continued, 'in obtaining one thing which we shall find very useful in inducing the Prince to listen to what we have to say to him about his father. You may not know it, but about the time when the King was thrown into the well, the seal of the kingdom mysteriously disappeared and a new one had to be cut.

'Knowing that you were going to summon me to discuss this case, I went down into the well at dawn this morning, and found the missing seal on the body of the King. Here it is, and now we must lay our plans to work on the mind of the son for the deliverance of the father. To-morrow I hear that the Prince is going out hunting on the neighbouring hills. In one of the valleys there is a temple to the Goddess of Mercy, and if you will take this seal and await his coming there, I promise you that I will find means to entice him to the shrine.'

Next morning the heir to the Throne of the 'Kingdom of the Black Flower' set out with a noisy retinue to have a day's hunting on the well-wooded hills overlooking the capital. They had scarcely reached the hunting grounds when great excitement was caused by the sudden appearance of a remarkable-looking hare. It was decidedly larger than an ordinary hare, but the curious feature about it was its colour, which was as white as the driven snow.

No sooner had the hounds caught sight of it, than with loud barkings and bayings they dashed madly in pursuit. The hare, however, did not seem to show any terror, but with graceful bounds that carried it rapidly over the ground, it easily outdistanced the fleetest of its pursuers. It appeared, indeed, as though it were thoroughly enjoying the facility with which it could outrun the dogs, while the latter grew more and more excited as they always saw the quarry before them and yet could never get near enough to lay hold upon it.

Another extraordinary thing was that this hare did not seem anxious to escape. It took no advantage of undergrowth or of clumps of trees to hide the direction in which it was going. It managed also to keep constantly in view of the whole field; and when it had to make sudden turns in the natural windings of the road which led to a valley in the distance, where there stood a famous temple, it hesitated for a moment and allowed the baying hounds to come perilously near, before it darted off with the speed of lightning and left the dogs far behind it.

Little did the hunters dream that the beautiful animal which was giving them such an exciting chase was none other than the fairy Hing, who had assumed this disguise in order to bring the Prince to the lonely temple in the secluded valley, where, beyond the possibility of being spied upon by his father's murderer, the story of treachery could be told, and means be devised for his restoration to the throne.

Having arrived close to the temple, the mysterious hare vanished as suddenly as it had appeared, and not a trace was left to enable the dogs, which careered wildly round and round, to pick up the scent.

The Prince, who was a devoted disciple of the Goddess of Mercy, now dismounted and entered the temple, where he proceeded to burn incense before her shrine and in muttered tones to beseech her to send down blessings upon him.

After a time, he became considerably surprised to find that the presiding priest of the temple, instead of coming forward to attend upon him and to show him the courtesies due to his high position, remained standing in a corner where the shadows were darkest, his eyes cast upon the ground and with a most serious look overspreading his countenance.

Accordingly, when he had finished his devotions to the Goddess, the Prince approached the priest, and asked him in a kindly manner if anything was distressing him.

'Yes,' replied Hien-Chung, 'there is, and it is a subject which materially affects your Royal Highness. If you will step for a moment into my private room, I shall endeavour to explain to you the matter which has filled my mind with the greatest possible anxiety.'

When they entered the abbot's room, Hien-Chung handed the Prince a small box and asked him to open it and examine the article it contained.

Great was the Prince's amazement when he took it out and cast a hurried glance over it. A look of excitement passed over his face and he cried out, 'Why, this is the great seal of the kingdom which was lost three years ago, and of which no trace could ever be found! May I ask how it came into your possession and what reason you can give for not having restored it to the King, who has long wished to discover it?'

'The answer to that is a long one, your Highness, and to satisfy you, I must go somewhat into detail.'

Hien-Chung then told the Prince of the midnight visit his father had made him, and the tragic story of his murder by the man who was now posing as the King, and of his appeal to deliver him from the sorrows of the well in which he had been confined for three years.

'With regard to the finding of the seal,' he continued, 'my servant Hing, who is present, will describe how by the supernatural powers with which he is endowed, he descended the well only this very morning and discovered it on the body of your father.'

'We have this absolute proof,' he said, 'that the vision I saw only two nights ago was not some imagination of the brain, but that it was really the King who appealed to me to deliver him from the power of an enemy who seems bent upon his destruction.

'We must act, and act promptly,' he went on, 'for the man who is pretending to be the ruler of your kingdom is a person of unlimited ability, and as soon as he gets to know that his secret has been divulged, he will put into operation every art he possesses to frustrate our purpose.

'What I propose is that your Highness should send back the

greater part of your retinue to the palace, with an intimation to the effect that you are going to spend the night here in a special service to the Goddess, whose birthday it fortunately happens to be to-day. After night has fallen upon the city, Hing shall descend into the well and bring the body of your father here. You will then have all the proof you need of the truth of the matter, and we can devise plans as to our future action.'

A little after midnight, Hing having faithfully carried out the commission entrusted to him by Hien-Chung, arrived with the body of the King, which was laid with due ceremony and respect in one of the inner rooms of the temple. With his marvellous wonder-working powers and with the aid of invisible forces which he had been able to summon to his assistance, he had succeeded in transporting it from the wretched place where it had lain so long to the friendly temple of the Goddess of Mercy.

The Prince was deeply moved by the sight of his father's body. Fortunately it had suffered no change since the day when it was thrown to the bottom of the well. Not a sign of decay could be seen upon the King's noble features. It seemed as though he had but fallen asleep, and presently would wake up and talk to them as he used to do. The fact that in some mysterious way the soul had not been separated from the body accounted for its remarkable preservation. Nevertheless to all appearance the King was dead, and the great question now was how he could be brought back to life, so that he might be restored to his family and his kingdom.

'The time has come,' said Hien-Chung, 'when heroic measures will have to be used if the King is ever to live again. Two nights ago he made a passionate and urgent request to me to save him, for one of the gods informed him that I was the only man who could do so. So far, we have got him out of the grip of the demon that compassed his death, and now it lies with me to provide some antidote which shall bring back the vital forces and make him a living man once more.

'I have never had to do with such a serious case as this before, but I have obtained from the Patriarch of the Taoist Church a small vial of the Elixir of Life, which has the marvellous property of prolonging the existence of whoever drinks it. We shall try it on the King and, as there is no sign of vital decay, let us hope that it will be effective in restoring him to life.'

Turning to a desk that was kept locked, he brought out a small black earthenware bottle, from which he dropped a single drop of liquid on to the lips of the prostrate figure. In a few seconds a kind of rosy flush spread over the King's features. Another drop, and a look of life flashed over the pallid face. Still another, and after a short interval the eyes opened and looked with intelligence upon the group surrounding his couch. Still one more, and the King arose and asked how long he had been asleep, and how it came about that he was in this small room instead of being in his own palace.

He was soon restored to his family and to his position in the State, for the usurper after one or two feeble attempts to retain his power ignominiously fled from the country.

A short time after, Hien-Chung had a private interview with the King. 'I am anxious,' he said, 'that your Majesty should understand the reason why such a calamity came into your life.

'Some years ago without any just reason you put to death a Buddhist priest. You never showed any repentance for the great wrong you had done, and so the Goddess sent a severe drought upon your Kingdom. You still remained unrepentant, and then she sent one of her Ministers to afflict you, depriving you of your home and your royal power. The man who pushed you down the well was but carrying out the instructions he had received from the Goddess. Your stay down the well for three years was part of the punishment she had decreed for your offence, and when the time was up, I was given the authority to release you.

'Kings as well as their subjects are under the great law of righteousness, and if they violate it they must suffer like other men. I would warn your Majesty that unless you show some evidence that you have repented for taking away a man's life unjustly, other sorrows will most certainly fall upon you in the future.'

29

The Two Cats

(Arabic)

In former days there was an old woman, who lived in a hut more confined than the minds of the ignorant, and more dark than the tombs of misers. Her companion was a cat, from the mirror of whose imagination the appearance of bread had never been reflected, nor had she from friends or strangers ever heard its name. It was enough that she now and then scented a mouse, or observed the print of its feet on the floor; when, blessed by favouring stars or benignant fortune, one fell into her claws—

> 'She became like a beggar who discovers a treasure of gold;
> Her cheeks glowed with rapture, and past grief was consumed by present joy.'

This feast would last for a week or more; and while enjoying it she was wont to exclaim—

> 'Am I, O God, when I contemplate this, in a dream or awake?
> Am I to experience such prosperity after such adversity?'

But as the dwelling of the old woman was in general the mansion of famine to this cat, she was always complaining, and forming extravagant and fanciful schemes. One day, when reduced to extreme weakness, she, with much exertion, reached the top of the hut; when there she observed a cat stalking on the wall of a neighbour's house, which, like a fierce tiger, advanced with measured steps, and was so loaded with flesh that she could hardly raise her feet. The old woman's friend was amazed to see one of her own species so fat and sleek, and broke out into the following exclamation:—

> 'Your stately strides have brought you here at last; pray tell me from whence you come?
> From whence have you arrived with so lovely an appearance?
> You look as if from the banquet of the Khan of Khatai.
> Where have you acquired such a comeliness? And how came you by that glorious strength?'

The other answered, 'I am the Sultan's crumb-eater. Each morning, when they spread the convivial table, I attend at the palace, and there exhibit my address and courage. From among the rich meats and wheat-cakes I cull a few choice morsels; I then retire and pass my time till next day in delightful indolence.'

The old dame's cat requested to know what rich meat was, and what taste wheat-cakes had? 'As for me,' she added, in a melancholy tone, 'during my life I have neither eaten nor seen anything but the old woman's gruel and the flesh of mice.' The other, smiling, said, 'This accounts for the difficulty I find in distinguishing you from a spider. Your shape and stature is such as must make the whole generation of cats blush; and we must ever feel ashamed while you carry so miserable an appearance abroad.

> 'You certainly have the ears and tail of a cat,
> But in other respects you are a complete spider.

'Were you to see the Sultan's palace, and to smell his delicious viands, most undoubtedly those withered bones would be restored; you would receive new life; you would come from behind the curtain of invisibility into the plane of observation—

> 'When the perfume of his beloved passes over the tomb of a lover,
> Is it wonderful that his putrid bones should be re-animated?'

The old woman's cat addressed the other in the most supplicating manner: 'O my sister!' she exclaimed, 'have I not the sacred claims of a neighbour upon you? are we not linked in the ties of kindred? What prevents your giving a proof of friendship, by taking me with you when next you visit the palace? Perhaps from your favour plenty may flow to me, and from your patronage I may attain dignity and honour.

> 'Withdraw not from the friendship of the honourable;
> Abandon not the support of the elect.'

The heart of the Sultan's crumb-eater was melted by this pathetic address; she promised her new friend should accompany her on the next visit to the palace. The latter, overjoyed, went down immediately from the terrace, and communicated every particular to the old woman, who addressed her with the following counsel:—

'Be not deceived, my dearest friend, with the worldly language you have listened to; abandon not your corner of content, for the cup of the covetous is only to be filled by the dust of the grave, and the eye of cupidity and hope can only be closed by the needle of mortality and the thread of fate.

> 'It is content that makes men rich;
> Mark this, ye avaricious, who traverse the world:
> He neither knows nor pays adoration to his God
> Who is dissatisfied with his condition and fortune.'

But the expected feast had taken such possession of poor puss's imagination, that the medicinal counsel of the old woman was thrown away.

> 'The good advice of all the world is like wind in a cage,
> Or water in a sieve, when bestowed on the headstrong.'

To conclude: next day, accompanied by her companion, the half-starved cat hobbled to the Sultan's palace. Before this unfortunate wretch came, as it is decreed that the covetous shall be disappointed, an extraordinary event had occurred, and, owing to her evil destiny, the water of disappointment was poured on the flame of her immature ambition. The case was this: a whole legion of cats had the day before surrounded the feast, and made so much noise that they disturbed the guests; and in consequence the Sultan had ordered that some archers armed with bows from Tartary should, on this day, be concealed, and that whatever cat advanced into the field of valour, covered with the shield of audacity, should, on eating the first morsel, be overtaken with their arrows. The old dame's puss was not aware of this order. The moment the flavour of the viands reached her, she flew like an eagle to the place of her prey.

Scarcely had the weight of a mouthful been placed in the scale to balance her hunger, when a heart-dividing arrow pierced her breast.

A stream of blood rushed from the wound.
She fled, in dread of death, after having exclaimed,
'Should I escape from this terrific archer, I will be satisfied
with my mouse and the miserable hut of my old mistress.
My soul rejects the honey if accompanied by the sting.
Content, with the most frugal fare, is preferable.'

30

The Indigent Brahman

(Indian)

There was a Brahman who had a wife and four children. He was very poor. With no resources in the world, he lived chiefly on the benefactions of the rich. His gains were considerable when marriages were celebrated or funeral ceremonies were performed; but as his parishioners did not marry every day, neither did they die every day, he found it difficult to make the two ends meet. His wife often rebuked him for his inability to give her adequate support, and his children often went about naked and hungry. But though poor he was a good man. He was diligent in his devotions; and there was not a single day in his life in which he did not say his prayers at stated hours. His tutelary deity was the goddess Durga, the consort of Siva, the creative Energy of the Universe. On no day did he either drink water or taste food till he had written in red ink the name of Durga at least one hundred and eight times; while throughout the day he incessantly uttered the ejaculation, 'O Durga! O Durga! have mercy upon me.' Whenever he felt anxious on account of his poverty and his inability to support his wife and children, he groaned out—'Durga! Durga! Durga!'

One day, being very sad, he went to a forest many miles distant from the village in which he lived, and indulging his grief wept bitter tears. He prayed in the following manner:—'O Durga! O Mother Bhagavati! Wilt thou not make an end of my misery? Were I alone in the world, I should not have been sad on account of poverty; but thou hast given me a wife and children. Give me, O Mother, the means to support them.' It so happened that on that day and on that very spot the god Siva and his wife Durga were taking their morning walk. The goddess Durga, on seeing the Brahman at a distance, said to her divine husband—'O Lord of Kailas! do you see that Brahman? He is always taking my name on his lips and offering the prayer that I should deliver him out of his troubles. Can we not, my lord, do something for the poor Brahman, oppressed as he is with the cares of a growing family? We should give him enough to make him comfortable. As the poor man and his family have never enough to eat, I propose that you give him a handi1 which should yield him an inexhaustible supply of *mudki* (fried paddy boiled dry in treacle or sugar).' The lord of Kailas readily agreed to the proposal of his divine consort, and by his decree created on the spot a handi possessing the required quality. Durga then, calling the Brahman to her, said,—'O Brahman! I have often thought of your pitiable case. Your repeated prayers have at last moved my compassion. Here is a *handi* (an earthen pot) for you. When you turn it upside down and shake it, it will pour down a never-ceasing shower of the finest mudki, which will not end till you restore the handi to its proper position. Yourself, your wife, and your children can eat as much mudki as you like, and you can also sell as much as you like.' The Brahman, delighted beyond measure at obtaining so inestimable a treasure, made obeisance to the goddess, and, taking the handi in his hand, proceeded towards his house as fast as his legs could carry him. But he had not gone many yards when he thought of testing the efficacy of the wonderful vessel. Accordingly he turned the handi upside down and shook it, when, lo, and behold! A quantity of the finest mudki he had ever seen fell to the ground. He tied the sweetmeat in his sheet and walked on. It was now noon, and the Brahman was hungry; but he could not eat without his ablutions and his prayers. As he saw in the way an inn, and not far from it a tank, he purposed to halt there that he might bathe, say his prayers, and then eat the much-desired mudki. The Brahman sat at the innkeeper's shop, put the handi near him, smoked tobacco, besmeared his body with mustard oil, and before proceeding to bathe in the adjacent tank gave the handi in charge to the innkeeper, begging him again and again to take especial care of it.

When the Brahman went to his bath and his devotions, the innkeeper thought it strange that he should be so careful as to the safety of his earthen vessel. There must be something valuable in the handi, he thought, otherwise why should the Brahman take so much thought about it? His curiosity being excited he opened the handi, and to his surprise found that it contained nothing. What can be the meaning of this? thought the innkeeper within himself. Why should the Brahman care so much for an empty handi? He took up the vessel, and began to examine it carefully; and when, in the course of examination, he turned the handi upside down, a quantity of the finest mudki fell from it, and went on falling without intermission. The innkeeper called his wife and children to witness this unexpected stroke of good fortune. The showers of the sugared fried paddy were so copious that they filled all the vessels and jars of the innkeeper. He resolved to appropriate to himself this precious handi, and accordingly put in its place another handi of the same size and make. The ablutions and devotions of the Brahman being now over, he came to the shop in wet clothes reciting holy texts of the Vedas. Putting on dry clothes, he wrote on a sheet of paper the name of Durga one hundred and eight times in red ink; after which he broke his fast on the mudki his handi had already given him. Thus refreshed, and being about to resume his journey homewards, he called for his handi, which the innkeeper delivered to him, adding—'There, sir, is your handi; it is just where you put it; no one has touched it.' The Brahman, without suspecting anything, took up the handi and proceeded on his journey; and as he walked on, he congratulated himself on his singular good fortune. 'How agreeably,' he thought within himself, 'will my poor wife be surprised! How greedily the children will devour the mudki of heaven's own manufacture! I shall soon become rich, and lift up my head with the best of them all.' The pains of travelling were considerably alleviated by these joyful anticipations. He reached his house, and calling his wife and children, said—'Look now at what I have brought. This handi that you see is an unfailing source of wealth and contentment. You will see what a stream of the finest mudki will flow from it when I turn it upside down.' The Brahman's good wife, hearing of mudki falling from the handi unceasingly, thought that her husband must have gone mad; and she was confirmed in her opinion when she found that nothing fell from the vessel though it was turned upside down again and again. Overwhelmed with grief, the Brahman concluded that the innkeeper must have played a trick with him; he must have stolen the handi Durga had given him, and put a common one in its stead. He went back the next day to the innkeeper, and charged him with having changed his handi. The innkeeper put on a fit of anger, expressed surprise at the Brahman's impudence in charging him with theft, and drove him away from his shop.

The Brahman then bethought himself of an interview with the goddess Durga who had given him the handi, and accordingly went to the forest where he had met her. Siva and Durga again favoured the Brahman with an interview. Durga said—'So, you have lost the handi I gave you. Here is another, take it and make good use of it.' The Brahman, elated with joy, made obeisance to the divine couple, took up the vessel, and went on his way. He had not gone far when he turned it upside down, and shook it in order to see whether any mudki would fall from it. Horror of horrors! Instead of sweetmeats about a score of demons, of gigantic size and grim visage, jumped out of the handi, and began to belabour the astonished Brahman with blows, fisticuffs and kicks. He had the presence of mind to turn up the handi and to cover it, when the demons forthwith disappeared. He concluded that this new handi had been given him only for the punishment of the innkeeper. He accordingly went to the innkeeper, gave him the new handi in charge, begged of him carefully to keep it till he returned from his ablutions and prayers. The innkeeper, delighted with this second godsend, called his wife and children, and said—'This is another handi brought here by the same Brahman who brought the handi of mudki. This time, I hope, it is not mudki but *sandesa* (a sort of sweetmeat made of curds and sugar). Come, be ready with baskets and vessels, and I'll turn the handi upside down and shake it.' This was no sooner done than scores of fierce demons started up, who caught hold of the innkeeper and his family and belaboured them mercilessly. They also began upsetting the shop, and would have completely destroyed it, if the victims had not besought the Brahman, who had by this time returned from his ablutions, to show mercy to them and send away the terrible demons. The Brahman acceded to the innkeeper's request, he dismissed the demons by shutting up the vessel; he got the former handi, and with the two handis went to his native village.

On reaching home the Brahman shut the door of his house, turned the mudki-handi upside down, and shook it; the result was an unceasing stream of the finest mudki that any confectioner in the country could produce. The man, his wife, and their children devoured the sweetmeat to their hearts' content; all the available earthen pots and pans of the house were filled with it; and the Brahman resolved the next day to turn confectioner, to open a shop in his house, and sell mudki. On the very day the shop was opened, the whole village came to the Brahman's house to buy the wonderful mudki. They had never seen such mudki in their life, it was so sweet, so white, so large, so luscious; no confectioner in the village or any town in the country had ever manufactured anything like it. The reputation of the Brahman's mudki extended, in a few days, beyond the bounds of the village, and people came from remote parts to purchase it. Cartloads of the sweetmeat were sold every day, and the Brahman in a short time became very rich. He built a large brick house, and lived like a nobleman of the land. Once, however, his property was about to go to wreck and ruin. His children one day by mistake shook the wrong handi, when a large number of demons dropped down and caught hold of the Brahman's wife and children and were striking them mercilessly, when happily the Brahman came into the house and turned up the handi. In order to prevent a similar catastrophe in future, the Brahman shut up the demon-handi in a private room to which his children had no access.

Pure and uninterrupted prosperity, however, is not the lot of mortals; and though the demon-handi was put aside, what security was there that an accident might not befall the mudki-handi? One day, during the absence of the Brahman and his wife from the house, the children decided upon shaking the handi; but as each of them wished to enjoy the pleasure of shaking it there was a general struggle to get it, and in the mêlée the handi fell to the ground and broke. It is needless to say that the Brahman, when on reaching home he heard of the disaster, became inexpressibly sad. The children were of course well cudgelled, but no flogging of children could replace the magical handi. After some days he again went to the forest, and offered many a prayer for Durga's favour. At last Siva and Durga again appeared to him, and heard how the handi had been broken. Durga gave him another handi, accompanied with the following caution—'Brahman, take care of this handi; if you again break it or lose it, I'll not give you another.' The Brahman made obeisance, and went away to his house at one stretch without halting anywhere. On reaching home he shut the door of his house, called his wife to him, turned the handi upside down, and began to shake it. They were only expecting mudki to drop from it, but instead of mudki a perennial stream of beautiful sandesa issued from it. And such sandesa! No confectioner of Burra Bazar ever made its like. It was more the food of gods than of men. The Brahman forthwith set up a shop for selling sandesa, the fame of which soon drew crowds of customers from all parts of the country. At all festivals, at all marriage feasts, at all funeral celebrations, at all Pujas, no one bought any other sandesa than the Brahman's. Every day, and every hour, many jars of gigantic size, filled with the delicious sweetmeat, were sent to all parts of the country.

The wealth of the Brahman excited the envy of the Zemindar of the village, who, having heard that the sandesa was not manufactured but dropped from a handi, devised a plan for getting possession of the miraculous vessel. At the celebration of his son's marriage he held a great feast, to which were invited hundreds of people. As many mountain-loads of sandesa would be required for the purpose, the Zemindar proposed that the Brahman should bring the magical handi to the house in which the feast was held. The Brahman at first refused to take it there; but as the Zemindar insisted on its being carried to his own house, he reluctantly consented to take it there. After many Himalayas of sandesa had been shaken out, the handi was taken possession of by the Zemindar, and the Brahman was insulted and driven out of the house. The Brahman, without giving vent to anger in the least, quietly went to his house, and taking the demon-handi in his hand, came back to the door of the Zemindar's house. He turned the handi upside down and shook it, on which a hundred demons started up as from the vasty deep and enacted a scene which it is impossible to describe. The hundreds of guests that had been bidden to the feast were caught hold of by the unearthly visitants and beaten; the women were dragged by their hair from the Zenana and dashed about amongst the men; while the big and burly Zemindar was driven about from room to room like a bale of cotton. If the demons had been allowed to do their will only for a few minutes longer, all the men would have been killed, and the very house razed to the ground. The Zemindar fell prostrate at the feet of the Brahman and begged for mercy. Mercy was shown him, and the demons were removed. After that the Brahman was no more disturbed by the Zemindar or by any one else; and he lived many years in great happiness and enjoyment.

> *Thus my story endeth,*
> *The Natiya-thorn withereth, etc.*

31

How We Got the Name 'Spider Tales'

(West African)

In the olden days all the stories which men told were stories of Nyankupon, the chief of the gods. Spider, who was very conceited, wanted the stories to be told about him.

Accordingly, one day he went to Nyankupon and asked that, in future, all tales told by men might be Anansi stories, instead of Nyankupon stories. Nyankupon agreed, on one condition. He told Spider (or Anansi) that he must bring him three things: the first was a jar full of live bees, the second was a boa-constrictor, and the third a tiger. Spider gave his promise.

He took an earthen vessel and set out for a place where he knew were numbers of bees. When he came in sight of the bees he began saying to himself, 'They will not be able to fill this jar'—'Yes, they will be able'—'No, they will not be able,' until the bees came up to him and said, 'What are you talking about, Mr Anansi?' He thereupon explained to them that Nyankupon and he had had a great dispute. Nyankupon had said the bees could not fly into the jar—Anansi had said they could. The bees immediately declared that of course they could fly into the jar—which they at once did. As soon as they were safely inside, Anansi sealed up the jar and sent it off to Nyankupon.

Next day he took a long stick and set out in search of a boa-constrictor. When he arrived at the place where one lived he began speaking to himself again. 'He will just be as long as this stick'—'No, he will not be so long as this'—'Yes, he will be as long as this.' These words he repeated several times, till the boa came out and asked him what was the matter. 'Oh, we have been having a dispute in Nyankupon's town about you. Nyankupon's people say you are not as long as this stick. I say you are. Please let me measure you by it.' The boa innocently laid himself out straight, and Spider lost no time in tying him on to the stick from end to end. He then sent him to Nyankupon.

The third day he took a needle and thread and sewed up his eye. He then set out for a den where he knew a tiger lived. As he approached the place he began to shout and sing so loudly that the tiger came out to see what was the matter. 'Can you not see?' said Spider. 'My eye is sewn up and now I can see such wonderful things that I must sing about them.' 'Sew up my eyes,' said the tiger, 'then I too can see these surprising sights.' Spider immediately did so. Having thus made the tiger helpless, he led him straight to Nyankupon's house. Nyankupon was amazed at Spider's cleverness in fulfilling the three conditions. He immediately gave him permission for the future to call all the old tales Anansi tales.

32

Dogedog

(Filipino)

Dogedog had always been very lazy, and now that his father and mother were dead and he had no one to care for him, he lived very poorly. He had little to eat. His house was old and small and so poor that it had not even a floor. Still he would rather sit all day and idle away his time than to work and have more things.

One day, however, when the rainy season was near at hand, Dogedog began thinking how cold he would be when the storms came, and he felt so sorry for himself that he decided to make a floor in his house.

Wrapping some rice in a banana leaf for his dinner, he took his long knife and went to the forest to cut some bamboo. He hung the bundle of rice in a tree until he should need it; but while he was working a cat came and ate it. When the hungry man came for his dinner, there was none left. Dogedog went back to his miserable little house which looked forlorn to him even, now that he had decided to have a floor.

The next day he went again to the forest and hung his rice in the tree as he did before, but again the cat came and ate it. So the man had to go home without any dinner.

The third day he took the rice, but this time he fixed a trap in the tree, and when the cat came it was caught.

'Now I have you!' cried the man when he found the cat; 'and I shall kill you for stealing my rice.'

'Oh, do not kill me,' pleaded the cat, 'and I will be of some use to you.'

So Dogedog decided to spare the cat's life, and he took it home and tied it near the door to guard the house.

Some time later when he went to look at it, he was very much surprised to find that it had become a cock.

'Now I can go to the cock-fight at Magsingal,' cried the man. And he was very happy, for he had much rather do that than work.

Thinking no more of getting wood for his floor, he started out at once for Magsingal with the cock under his arm. As he was crossing a river he met an alligator which called out to him:

'Where are you going, Dogedog?'

'To the cock-fight at Magsingal,' replied the man as he fondly stroked the rooster.

'Wait, and I will go with you,' said the alligator; and he drew himself out of the water.

The two walking along together soon entered a forest where they met a deer and it asked:

'Where are you going, Dogedog?'

'To the cock-fight at Magsingal,' said the man.

'Wait and I will go with you,' said the deer; and he also joined them.

By and by they met a mound of earth that had been raised by the ants, and they would have passed without noticing it had it not inquired:

'Where are you going, Dogedog?'

'To the cock-fight at Magsingal,' said the man once more; and the mound of earth joined them.

The company then hurried on, and just as they were leaving the forest, they passed a big tree in which was a monkey.

'Where are you going, Dogedog?' shrieked the monkey. And without waiting for an answer he scrambled down the tree and followed them.

As the party walked along they talked together, and the alligator said to Dogedog:

'If any man wants to dive into the water, I can stay under longer than he.'

Then the deer, not to be outdone, said:

'If any man wants to run, I can run faster.'

The mound of earth, anxious to show its strength, said:

'If any man wants to wrestle, I can beat him.'

And the monkey said:

'If any man wants to climb, I can go higher.'

They reached Magsingal in good time and the people were ready for the fight to begin. When Dogedog put his rooster, which had been a cat, into the pit, it killed the other cock at once, for it used its claws like a cat.

The people brought more roosters and wagered much money, but Dogedog's cock killed all the others until there was not one left in Magsingal, and Dogedog won much money. Then they went outside the town and brought all the cocks they could find, but not one could win over that of Dogedog.

When the cocks were all dead, the people wanted some other sport, so they brought a man who could stay under water for a long time, and Dogedog made him compete with the alligator. But after a while the man had to come up first. Then they brought a swift runner and he raced with the deer, but the man was left far behind. Next they looked around until they found a very large man who was willing to contend with the mound of earth, but after a hard struggle the man was thrown.

Finally they brought a man who could climb higher than anyone else, but the monkey went far above him, and he had to give up.

All these contests had brought much money to Dogedog, and now he had to buy two horses to carry his sacks of silver. As soon as he reached home, he bought the house of a very rich man and went to live in it. And he was very happy, for he did not have to work any more.

33

Aponibolinayen

(Filipino)

The most beautiful girl in all the world was Aponibolinayen of Nalpangan. Many young men had come to her brother, Aponibalagen, to ask for her hand in marriage, but he had refused them all, for he awaited one who possessed great power. Then it happened that the fame of her beauty spread over all the world till it reached even to Adasen; and in that place there lived a man of great power named Gawigawen.

Now Gawigawen, who was a handsome man, had sought among all the pretty girls but never, until he heard of the great beauty of Aponibolinayen, had he found one whom he wished to wed. Then he determined that she should be his wife; and he begged his mother to help him win her. So Dinawagen, the mother of Gawigawen, took her hat which looked like a sunbeam and set out at once for Nalpangan; and when she arrived there she was greeted by Ebang, the mother of the lovely maiden, who presently began to prepare food for them.

She put the pot over the fire, and when the water boiled she broke up a stick and threw the pieces into the pot, and immediately they became fish. Then she brought basi in a large jar, and Dinawagen, counting the notches in the rim, perceived that the jar had been handed down through nine generations. They ate and drank together, and after they had finished the meal, Dinawagen told Aponibalagen of her son's wishes, and asked if he was willing that his sister should marry Gawigawen. Aponibalagen, who had heard of the power of the suitor, at once gave his consent. And Dinawagen departed for home, leaving a gold cup as an engagement present.

Gawigawen was watching at the door of his house for his mother's return, and when she told him of her success, he was so happy that he asked all the people in the town to go with him the next day to Nalpangan to arrange the amount he must pay for his bride.

Now the people of Nalpangan wanted a great price for this girl who was so beautiful, and the men of the two towns debated for a long time before they could come to an agreement. Finally, however, it was decided that Gawigawen should fill the spirit house eighteen times with valuable things; and when he had done this, they were all satisfied and went to the yard where they danced and beat on the copper gongs. All the pretty girls danced their best, and one who wore big jars about her neck made more noise than the others as she danced, and the jars sang 'Kitol, kitol, kanitol; inka, inka, inkatol.'

But when Aponibolinayen, the bride of Gawigawen, came down out of the house to dance, the sunshine vanished, so beautiful was she; and as she moved about, the river came up into the town, and striped fish bit at her heels.

For three months the people remained here feasting and dancing, and then early one morning they took Aponibolinayen to her new home in Adasen. The trail that led from one town to the other had become very beautiful in the meantime: the grass and trees glistened with bright lights, and the waters of the tiny streams dazzled the eyes with their brightness as Aponibolinayen waded across. When they reached the spring of Gawigawen, they found that it, too, was more beautiful than ever before. Each grain of sand had become a bead, and the place where the women set their jars when they came to dip water had become a big dish.

Then said Aponibalagen to his people, 'Go tell Gawigawen to bring an old man, for I want to make a spring for Aponibolinayen.'

So an old man was brought and Aponibalagen cut off his head and put it in the ground, and sparkling water bubbled up. The body he made into a tree to shade his sister when she came to dip water, and the drops of blood as they touched the ground were changed into valuable beads. Even the path from the spring to the house was covered with big plates, and everything was made beautiful for Aponibolinayen.

Now during all this time Aponibolinayen had kept her face covered so that she had never seen her husband, for although he was a handsome man, one of the pretty girls who was jealous of the bride had told her that he had three noses, and she was afraid to look at him.

After her people had all returned to their homes, she grew very unhappy, and when her mother-in-law commanded her to cook she had to feel her way around, for she would not uncover her face. Finally she became so sad that she determined to run away. One night when all were asleep, she used magical power and changed herself into oil. Then she slid through the bamboo floor and made her escape without anyone seeing her.

On and on she went until she came to the middle of the

jungle, and then she met a wild rooster who asked her where she was going.

'I am running away from my husband,' replied Aponibolinayen, 'for he has three noses and I do not want to live with him.'

'Oh,' said the rooster, 'some crazy person must have told you that. Do not believe it. Gawigawen is a handsome man, for I have often seen him when he comes here to snare chickens.'

But Aponibolinayen paid no heed to the rooster, and she went on until she reached a big tree where perched a monkey, and he also asked where she was going.

'I am running away from my husband,' answered the girl, 'for he has three noses and I do not want to live with him.'

'Oh, do not believe that,' said the monkey. 'Someone who told you that must have wanted to marry him herself, for he is a handsome man.'

Still Aponibolinayen went on until she came to the ocean, and then, as she could go no farther, she sat down to rest. As she sat there pondering what she should do, a carabao came along, and thinking that she would ride a while she climbed up on its back. No sooner had she done so than the animal plunged into the water and swam with her until they reached the other side of the great ocean.

There they came to a large orange tree, and the carabao told her to eat some of the luscious fruit while he fed on the grass nearby. As soon as he had left her, however, he ran straight to his master, Kadayadawan, and told him of the beautiful girl.

Kadayadawan was very much interested and quickly combed his hair and oiled it, put on his striped coat and belt, and went with the carabao to the orange tree. Aponibolinayen, looking down from her place in the tree, was surprised to see a man coming with her friend, the carabao, but as they drew near, she began talking with him, and soon they became acquainted. Before long, Kadayadawan had persuaded the girl to become his wife, and he took her to his home. From that time every night his house looked as if it was on fire, because of the beauty of his bride.

After they had been married for some time, Kadayadawan and Aponibolinayen decided to make a ceremony for the spirits, so they called the magic betel-nuts and oiled them and said to them,

'Go to all the towns and invite our relatives to come to the ceremony which we shall make. If they do not want to come, then grow on their knees until they are willing to attend.'

So the betel-nuts started in different directions and one went to Aponibalagen in Nalpangan and said,

'Kadayadawan is making a ceremony for the spirits, and I have come to summon you to attend.'

'We cannot go,' said Aponibalagen, 'for we are searching for my sister who is lost.'

'You must come,' replied the betel-nut, 'or I shall grow on your knee,'

'Grow on my pig,' answered Aponibalagen; so the betel-nut went on to the pig's back and grew into a tall tree, and it became so heavy that the pig could not carry it, but squealed all the time.

Then Aponibalagen, seeing that he must obey, said to the betel-nut,

'Get off my pig, and we will go.'

The betel-nut got off the pig's back, and the people started for the ceremony. When they reached the river, Gawigawen was there waiting to cross, for the magic nuts had forced him to go also. Then Kadayadawan, seeing them, sent more betel-nuts to the river, and the people were carried across by the nuts.

As soon as they reached the town the dancing began, and while Gawigawen was dancing with Aponibolinayen he seized her and put her in his belt. Kadayadawan, who saw this, was so angry that he threw his spear and killed Gawigawen. Then Aponibolinayen escaped and ran into the house, and her husband brought his victim back to life, and asked him why he had seized the wife of his host. Gawigawen explained that she was his wife who had been lost, and the people were very much surprised, for they had not recognized her at first.

Then all the people discussed what should be done to bring peace between the two men, and it was finally decided that Kadayadawan must pay both Aponibalagen and Gawigawen the price that was first demanded for the beautiful girl.

After this was done all were happy; and the guardian spirit of Kadayadawan gave them a golden house in which to live.

34

The Plucky Maiden

(Korean)

Han Myong-hoi was a renowned Minister of the Reign of Se-jo (A.D. 1455–1468). The King appreciated and enjoyed him greatly, and there was no one of the Court who could surpass him for influence and royal favour. Confident in his position, Han did as he pleased, wielding absolute power. At that time, like grass before the wind, the world bowed at his coming; no one dared utter a word of remonstrance.

When Han went as governor to Pyong-an Province he did all manner of lawless things. Any one daring to cross his wishes in the least was dealt with by torture and death. The whole Province feared him as they would a tiger.

On a certain day Governor Han, hearing that the Deputy Prefect of Son-chon had a very beautiful daughter, called the Deputy, and said, 'I hear that you have a very beautiful daughter, whom I would like to make my concubine. When I am on my official rounds shortly, I shall expect to stop at your town and take her. So be ready for me.'

The Deputy, alarmed, said, 'How can your Excellency say that your servant's contemptible daughter is beautiful? Some one has reported her wrongly. But since you so command, how can I do but accede gladly?' So he bowed, said his farewell, and went home.

On his return his family noticed that his face was clouded with anxiety, and the daughter asked why it was. 'Did the Governor call you, father?' asked she; 'and why are you so anxious? Tell me, please.' At first, fearing that she would be disturbed, he did not reply, but her repeated questions forced him, so that he said, 'I am in trouble on your account,' and then told of how the Governor wanted her for his concubine. 'If I had refused I would have been killed, so I yielded; but a gentleman's daughter being made a concubine is a disgrace unheard of.'

The daughter made light of it and laughed. 'Why did you not think it out better than that, father? Why should a grown man lose his life for the sake of a girl? Let the daughter go. By losing one daughter and saving your life, you surely do better than saving your daughter and losing your life. One can easily see where the greater advantage lies. A daughter does not count; give her over, that's all. Don't for a moment think otherwise, just put away your distress and anxiety. We women, every one of us, are under the ban, and such things are decreed by Fate. I shall accept without any opposition, so please have no anxiety. It is settled now, and you, father, must yield and follow. If you do so all will be well.'

The father sighed, and said in reply, 'Since you seem so willing, my mind is somewhat relieved.' But from this time on the whole house was in distress. The girl alone seemed perfectly unmoved, not showing the slightest sign of fear. She laughed as usual, her light and happy laugh, and her actions seemed wonderfully free.

In a little the Governor reached Son-chon on his rounds. He then called the Deputy, and said, 'Make ready your daughter for to-morrow and all the things needed.' The Deputy came home and made preparation for the so-called wedding. The daughter said, 'This is not a real wedding; it is only the taking of a concubine, but still, make everything ready in the way of refreshments and ceremony as for a real marriage.' So the father did as she requested.

On the day following the Governor came to the house of the Deputy. He was not dressed in his official robes, but came simply in the dress and hat of a commoner. When he went into the inner quarters he met the daughter; she stood straight before him. Her two hands were lifted in ceremonial form, but instead of holding a fan to hide her face she held a sword before her. She was very pretty. He gave a great start of surprise, and asked the meaning of the knife that she held. She ordered her nurse to reply, who said, 'Even though I am an obscure countrywoman, I do not forget that I am born of the gentry; and though your Excellency is a high Minister of State, still to take me by force is an unheard-of dishonour. If you take me as your real and true wife I'll serve you with all my heart, but if you are determined to take me as a concubine I shall die now by this sword. For that reason I hold it. My life rests on one word from your Excellency. Speak it, please, before I decide.'

The Governor, though a man who observed no ceremony and never brooked a question, when he saw how beautiful and how determined this maiden was, fell a victim to her at once, and said, 'If you so decide, then, of course, I'll make you my real wife.'

Her answer was, 'If you truly mean it, then please withdraw and write out the certificate; send the gifts; provide the goose; dress in the proper way; come, and let us go through the required ceremony; drink the pledge-glass, and wed.'

The Governor did as she suggested, carried out the forms to the letter, and they were married.

She was not only a very pretty woman, but upright and true of soul—a rare person indeed. The Governor took her home, loved her and held her dear. He had, however, a real wife before and concubines, but he set them all aside and fixed his affections on this one only. She remonstrated with him over his wrongs and unrighteous acts, and he listened and made improvement. The world took note of it, and praised her as a true and wonderful woman. She counted herself the real wife, but the first wife treated her as a concubine, and all the relatives said likewise that she could never be considered a real wife. At that time King Se-jo frequently, in the dress of a commoner, used to visit Han's house. Han entertained him royally with refreshments, which his wife used to bring and offer before him. He called her his 'little sister.' On a certain day King Se-jo, as he was accustomed, came to the house, and while he was drinking he suddenly saw the woman fall on her face before him. The King in surprise inquired as to what she could possibly mean by such an act. She then told all the story of her being taken by force and brought to Seoul. She wept while she said, 'Though I am from a far-distant part of the country I am of the gentry by ancestry, and my husband took me with all the required ceremonies of a wife, so that I ought not to be counted a concubine. But there is no law in this land by which a second real wife may be taken after a first real wife exists, so they call me a concubine, a matter of deepest disgrace. Please, your Majesty, take pity on me and decide my case.'

The King laughed, and said, 'This is a simple matter to settle; why should my little sister make so great an affair of it, and bow before me? I will decide your case at once. Come.' He then wrote out with his own hand a document making her a real wife, and her children eligible for the highest office. He wrote it, signed it, stamped it and gave it to her.

From that time on she was known as a real wife, in rank and standing equal to the first one. No further word was ever slightingly spoken, and her children shared in the affairs of State.

35

Lumabet

(Filipino, Bagobo)

Soon after people were created on the earth, there was born a child named Lumabet, who lived to be a very, very old man. He could talk when he was but one day old, and all his life he did wonderful things until the people came to believe that he had been sent by Manama, the Great Spirit.

When Lumabet was still a young man he had a fine dog, and he enjoyed nothing so much as taking him to the mountains to hunt. One day the dog noticed a white deer. Lumabet and his companions started in pursuit, but the deer was very swift and they could not catch it. On and on they went until they had gone around the world, and still the deer was ahead. One by one his companions dropped out of the chase, but Lumabet would not give up until he had the deer.

All the time he had but one banana and one *camote* (sweet potato) for food, but each night he planted the skins of these, and in the morning he found a banana tree with ripe fruit and a sweet potato large enough to eat. So he kept on until he had been around the world nine times, and he was an old man and his hair was grey. At last he caught the deer, and then he called all the people to a great feast, to see the animal.

While all were making merry, Lumabet told them to take a knife and kill his father. They were greatly surprised, but did as he commanded, and when the old man was dead, Lumabet waved his headband over him and he came to life again. Eight times they killed the old man at Lumabet's command, and the eighth time he was small like a little boy, for each time they had cut off some of his flesh. They all wondered very much at Lumabet's power, and they were certain that he was a god.

One morning some spirits came to talk with Lumabet, and after they had gone he called the people to come into his house.

'We cannot all come in,' said the people, 'for your house is small and we are many.'

'There is plenty of room,' said he; so all went in and to their surprise it did not seem crowded.

Then he told the people that he was going on a long journey and that all who believed he had great power could go with him, while all who remained behind would be changed into animals and *buso*. He started out, many following him, and it was as he said. For those that refused to go were immediately changed into animals and buso.

He led the people far away across the ocean to a place where the earth and the sky meet. When they arrived they saw that the sky moved up and down like a man opening and closing his jaws.

'Sky, you must go up,' commanded Lumabet.

But the sky would not obey. So the people could not go through. Finally Lumabet promised the sky that if he would let all the others through, he might have the last man who tried to pass. Agreeing to this, the sky opened and the people entered. But when near the last the sky shut down so suddenly that he caught not only the last man but also the long knife of the man before.

On that same day, Lumabet's son, who was hunting, did not know that his father had gone to the sky. When he was tired of the chase, he wanted to go to his father, so he leaned an arrow against a baliti tree and sat down on it. Slowly it began to go down and carried him to his father's place, but when he arrived he could find no people. He looked here and there and could find nothing but a gun made of gold. This made him very sorrowful and he did not know what to do until some white bees which were in the house said to him:

'You must not weep, for we can take you to the sky where your father is.'

So he did as they bade, and rode on the gun, and the bees flew away with him, until in three days they reached the sky.

Now, although most of the men who followed Lumabet were content to live in the sky, there was one who was very unhappy, and all the time he kept looking down on the land below. The spirits made fun of him and wanted to take out his intestines so that he would be like them and never die, but he was afraid and always begged to be allowed to go back home.

Finally Manama told the spirits to allow him to go, so they made a chain of the leaves of the karan grass and tied it to his legs. Then they let him down slowly head first, and when he reached the ground he was no longer a man but an owl.

36

The Goblins Turned to Stone

(Dutch)

When the cow came to Holland, the Dutch folks had more and better things to eat. Fields of wheat and rye took the place of forests. Instead of acorns and the meat of wild game, they now enjoyed milk and bread. The youngsters made pets of the calves and all the family lived under one roof. The cows had a happy time of it, because they were kept so clean, fed well, milked regularly, and cared for in winter.

By and by the Dutch learned to make cheese and began to eat it every day. They liked it, whether it was raw, cooked, toasted, sliced, or in chunks, or served with other good things. Even the foxes and wild creatures were very fond of the smell and taste of toasted cheese. They came at night close to the houses, often stealing the cheese out of the pantry. When a fox would not, or could not, be caught in a trap by any other bait, a bit of cooked cheese would allure him so that he was caught and his fur made use of.

When the people could not get meat, or fish, they had toasted bread and cheese, which in Dutch is 'geroostered brod met kaas.' Then they laughed, and named the new dish after whatever they pretended it was. It was just the same, as when they called goodies, made out of flour and sugar, 'nuts', 'fingers', 'calves' and 'lambs.' Even grown folks love to play and pretend things like children.

Soon, it became the fashion to have cheese parties. Men and women would sit around the fire, by the hour, nibbling the toast that had melted cheese poured over it. But after they had gone to bed, some of them dreamed.

Now some dreams may be pleasant, but cheese-dreams were not usually of this sort. The dreamer thought that a big she-horse had climbed upon the bed and sat down upon his stomach. Once there, the beast grinned hideously, snored, and pressed its hoofs down on the sleeper's breast, so that he could not breathe or speak. The feeling was a horrible one; but, just when the dreamer expected to choke, he seemed to jump off some high place, and come down somewhere, very far off. Then the animal ran away and the terrible dream was over.

This was called a nightmare, or in Dutch a 'nacht merrie.' 'Nacht' means night, and 'merrie' a filly or a mare. In the dream, it was not a small or a young horse, but always a big mare that squatted down on a man's stomach.

In those days, instead of seeking for the trouble inside, or asking whether there was any connection between nightmares and too hearty eating of cheese, the Dutch fathers laid it all on the goblins.

The goblins, or sooty elves, that used to live in Holland, were ugly, short fellows, very smart, quick in action and able to travel far in a second. They were first cousins to the kabouters. They had big heads, green eyes and split feet, like cows. They were so ugly, that they were ordered to live under ground and never come out during the day. If they did, they would be turned to stone.

The goblins had a bad reputation for mischief. They liked to have fun with human beings. They would listen to the conversation of people and then mock them by repeating the last word. That is the reason why echoes were called 'week klank,' or dwarf's talk.

Because these goblins were short, they envied men their greater stature and wanted to grow to the height of human beings. As they were not able of themselves to do this, they often sneaked into a house and snatched a child out of the cradle. In place of the stolen baby, one of their own wizened children was laid. That was the reason why many a poor little baby, that grew puny and thin, was called a 'wiseel-kind,' or changeling. When the sick baby could not get well, and medicine or care seemed to do no good, the mother thought that the goblins had taken away her own child.

It was only the female goblins that would change themselves into night mares and sit on the body of the dreamer. They usually came in through a hole or a crack; but if that person in the house could plug up the hole, or stop the crack, he could conquer the female goblin, and do what he pleased with her. If a man wanted to, he could make her his wife. So long as the hole was kept stopped up, by which the goblin entered, she made a good wife. If this crack was left open, or if the plug dropped out of the hole, the she-goblin was off and could never be found again.

The ruler of the goblins lived beneath the earth, as the king of the underworld. His palace was made of gold and glittered with gems. He had riches more than men could count. All the goblins and kabouters, who worked in the mines and at the forges and anvils, making swords, spears, bells, or jewels, obeyed him.

The most wonderful things about these dwarfs was the way in which they made themselves invisible, so that men were able to see neither the night mares nor the male goblins, while at their mischief. This was a little red cap which every goblin possessed, and which he was careful never to lose. The red cap acted like a snuffer on a candle, to put it out, and while under it, no goblin could be seen by mortal eyes.

Now it happened that one night, as a dear old lady lay dying on her bed, a middle-sized goblin, with his red cap on, came in through a crack into the room, and stood at the foot of her bed. Just for mischief and to frighten her by making himself visible, he took off his red cap.

When the old lady saw the imp, she cried out loudly:

'Go way, go way. Don't you know I belong to my Lord?'

But the goblin dwarf only laughed at her, with his green eyes.

Calling her daughter Alida, the old lady whispered in her ear:

'Bring me my wooden shoes.'

Rising up in her bed, the old lady hurled the heavy klomps, one after the other, at the goblin's head. At this, he started to get out through the crack, and away, but before his body was half out, Alida snatched his red cap away. Then she stuck a needle in his cloven foot that made him howl with pain. Alida looked at the crack through which he escaped and found it quite sooty.

Twirling the little red cap around on her forefinger, a brilliant thought struck her. She went and told the men her plan, and they agreed to it. This was to gather hundreds of farmers and townfolk, boys and men together, on the next moonlight night, and round up all the goblins in Drenthe. By pulling off their caps, and holding them till the sun rose, when they would be petrified, the whole brood could be exterminated.

So, knowing that the goblin would come the next night, to steal back his red cap, she left a note outside the crack, telling him to bring several hundred goblins to the great moor, or veldt. There, at a certain hour near midnight, he would find the red cap on a bush. With his companions, he could celebrate the return of the cap. In exchange for this, she asked the goblin to bring her a gold necklace.

The moonlight night came round and hundreds of the men of Drenthe gathered together. They were armed with horseshoes, and with witch-hazel and other plants, which are like poison to the sooty elves. They had also bits of parchment covered with runes, a strange kind of writing, and various charms which are supposed to be harmful to goblins. It was agreed to move together in a circle towards the centre, where the lady Alida was to hang the red cap upon a bush. Then, with a rush, the men were to snatch off all the goblins' caps, pulling and grabbing, whether they could see, or even feel anything, or not.

The placing of the red cap upon the bush in the centre, by the lady Alida, was the signal.

So, when the great round-up narrowed to a small space, the men began to grab, snatch and pull. Putting their hands out in the air, at the height of about a yard from the ground, they hustled and pushed hard. In a few minutes, hundreds of red caps were in their hands, and as many goblins became visible. They were, indeed, an ugly host.

Yet hundreds of other goblins escaped, with their caps on, and were still invisible. As they broke away in groups, however, they were seen, for in each bunch was one or more visible fellow, because he was capless. So the men divided into squads, to chase the imps a long distance, even to many distant places.

It was a most curious night battle. Here could be seen groups of men in a tussle with the goblins, many more of which, but by no means all, were made capless and visible.

The racket kept up till the sky in the east was gray. Had all the goblins run away, it would have been well with them. Hundreds of them did, but the others were so anxious to help their fellows, or to get back their own caps, fearing the disgrace of returning head bare to their king, and getting a good scolding, that the sun suddenly rose on them, before they knew it was day.

At the first level ray, the goblins were all turned to stone.

The treeless, desolate land, which, a moment before, was full of struggling goblins and men, became as quiet as the blue sky above. Nothing but some rounded rocks or stones, in groups, marked the spot where the bloodless battle of imps and men had been fought.

There, these stones, big and little, lie to this day. Among the buckwheat, and the potato blossoms of the summer, under the shadows and clouds, and whispering breezes of autumn, or covered with the snows of winter, they are seen on desolate heaths. Over some of them, oak trees, centuries old, have grown. Others are near, or among, the farmers' grain fields, or, not far from houses and barn-yards. The cows wander among them, knowing nothing of their past. And the goblins come no more.

37

The White Trout

(Irish)

There was wanst upon a time, long ago, a beautiful lady that lived in a castle upon the lake beyant, and they say she was promised to a king's son, and they wor to be married, when all of a sudden he was murthered, the crathur (Lord help us), and threwn into the lake above, and so, of course, he couldn't keep his promise to the fair lady,—and more's the pity.

Well, the story goes that she went out iv her mind, bekase av loosin' the king's son—for she was tendher-hearted, God help her, like the rest iv us!—and pined away after him, until at last, no one about seen her, good or bad; and the story wint that the fairies took her away.

Well, sir, in coorse o' time, the White Throut, God bless it, was seen in the sthrame beyant, and sure the people didn't know what to think av the crathur, seein' as how a *white* throut was never heard av afor, nor since; and years upon years the throut was there, just where you seen it this blessed minit, longer nor I can tell—aye throth, and beyant the memory o' th' ouldest in the village.

At last the people began to think it must be a fairy; for what else could it be?—and no hurt nor harm was iver put an the white trout, until some wicked sinners of sojers kem to these parts, and laughed at all the people, and gibed and jeered them for thinkin' o' the likes; and one o' them in partic'lar (bad luck to him; God forgi' me for saying it!) swore he'd catch the throut and ate it for his dinner—the blackguard!

Well, what would you think o' the villainy of the sojer? Sure enough he cotch the throut, and away wid him home, and puts an the fryin'-pan, and into it he pitches the purty little thing. The throut squeeled all as one as a Christian crathur, and, my dear, you'd think the sojer id split sides laughin'—for he was a harden'd villain; and when he thought one side was done, he turns it over to fry the other; and, what would you think, but the divil a taste of a burn was an it at all at all; and sure the sojer thought it was a *quare* throut that could not be briled. 'But,' says he, 'I'll give it another turn by-and-by,' little thinkin' what was in store for him, the haythen.

Well, when he thought that side was done he turns it agin, and lo and behould you, the divil a taste more done that side was nor the other. 'Bad luck to me,' says the sojer, 'but that bates the world,' says he; 'but I'll thry you agin, my darlint,' says he, 'as cunnin' as you think yourself;' and so with that he turns it over and over, but not a sign of the fire was on the purty throut. 'Well,' says the desperate villain—(for sure, sir, only he was a desperate villain *entirely*, he might know he was doing a wrong thing, seein' that all his endeavours was no good)—'Well,' says he, 'my jolly little throut, maybe you're fried enough, though you don't seem over well dress'd; but you may be better than you look, like a singed cat, and a tit-bit afther all,' says he; and with that he ups with his knife and fork to taste a piece o' the throut; but, my jew'l, the minit he puts his knife into the fish, there was a murtherin' screech, that you'd think the life id lave you if you hurd it, and away jumps the throut out av the fryin'-pan into the middle o' the flure; and an the spot where it fell, up riz a lovely lady—the beautifullest crathur that eyes ever seen, dressed in white, and a band o' goold in her hair, and a sthrame o' blood runnin' down her arm.

'Look where you cut me, you villain,' says she, and she held out her arm to him—and, my dear, he thought the sight id lave his eyes.

'Couldn't you lave me cool and comfortable in the river where you snared me, and not disturb me in my duty?' says she.

Well, he thrimbled like a dog in a wet sack, and at last he stammered out somethin', and begged for his life, and ax'd her ladyship's pardin, and said he didn't know she was on duty, or he was too good a sojer not to know betther nor to meddle wid her.

'I *was* on duty, then,' says the lady; 'I was watchin' for my true love that is comin' by wather to me,' says she, 'an' if he comes while I'm away, an' that I miss iv him, I'll turn you into a pinkeen, and I'll hunt you up and down for evermore, while grass grows or wather runs.'

Well the sojer thought the life id lave him, at the thoughts iv his bein' turned into a pinkeen, and begged for mercy; and with that says the lady—

'Renounce your evil coorses,' says she, 'you villain, or you'll repint it too late; be a good man for the futhur, and go to your duty reg'lar, and now,' says she, 'take me back and put me into the river again, where you found me.'

'Oh, my lady,' says the sojer, 'how could I have the heart to drownd a beautiful lady like you?'

But before he could say another word, the lady was vanished, and there he saw the little throut an the ground. Well he put it in a clean plate, and away he runs for the bare life, for fear her lover would come while she was away; and he run, and he run, even till he came to the cave agin, and threw the throut into the river. The minit he did, the wather was as red as blood for a little while, by rayson av the cut, I suppose, until the sthrame washed the stain away; and to this day there's a little red mark an the throut's side, where it was cut.

Well, sir, from that day out the sojer was an altered man, and reformed his ways, and went to his duty reg'lar, and fasted three times a-week—though it was never fish he tuk an fastin' days, for afther the fright he got, fish id never rest an his stomach—savin' your presence.

But anyhow, he was an altered man, as I said before, and in coorse o' time he left the army, and turned hermit at last; and they say he *used to pray evermore for the soul of the White Throut.*

38

The Ghost-Brahman

(Indian)

Once upon a time there lived a poor Brahman, who not being a Kulin, found it the hardest thing in the world to get married. He went to rich people and begged of them to give him money that he might marry a wife. And a large sum of money was needed, not so much for the expenses of the wedding, as for giving to the parents of the bride. He begged from door to door, flattered many rich folk, and at last succeeded in scraping together the sum needed. The wedding took place in due time; and he brought home his wife to his mother.

After a short time he said to his mother—'Mother, I have no means to support you and my wife; I must therefore go to distant countries to get money somehow or other. I may be away for years, for I won't return till I get a good sum. In the meantime I'll give you what I have; you make the best of it, and take care of my wife.' The Brahman receiving his mother's blessing set out on his travels. In the evening of that very day, a ghost assuming the exact appearance of the Brahman came into the house. The newly married woman, thinking it was her husband, said to him—'How is it that you have returned so soon? You said you might be away for years; why have you changed your mind?' The ghost said—'To-day is not a lucky day, I have therefore returned home; besides, I have already got some money.' The mother did not doubt but that it was her son. So the ghost lived in the house as if he was its owner, and as if he was the son of the old woman and the husband of the young woman. As the ghost and the Brahman were exactly like each other in everything, like two peas, the people in the neighbourhood all thought that the ghost was the real Brahman.

After some years the Brahman returned from his travels; and what was his surprise when he found another like him in the house. The ghost said to the Brahman—'Who are you? What business have you to come to my house?' 'Who am I?' replied the Brahman, 'let me ask who you are. This is my house; that is my mother, and this is my wife.' The ghost said—'Why herein is a strange thing. Every one knows that this is my house, that is my wife, and yonder is my mother; and I have lived here for years. And you pretend this is your house, and that woman is your wife. Your head must have got turned, Brahman.' So saying the ghost drove away the Brahman from his house. The Brahman became mute with wonder. He did not know what to do. At last he bethought himself of going to the king and of laying his case before him. The king saw the ghost-Brahman as well as the Brahman, and the one was the picture of the other; so he was in a fix, and did not know how to decide the quarrel.

Day after day the Brahman went to the king and besought him to give him back his house, his wife, and his mother; and the king, not knowing what to say every time, put him off to the following day. Every day the king tells him to—'Come to-morrow'; and every day the Brahman goes away from the palace weeping and striking his forehead with the palm of his hand, and saying—'What a wicked world this is! I am driven from my own house, and another fellow has taken possession of my house and of my wife! And what a king this is! He does not do justice.'

Now, it came to pass that as the Brahman went away every day from the court outside the town, he passed a spot at which a great many cowboys used to play. They let the cows graze on the meadow, while they themselves met together under a large tree to play. And they played at royalty. One cowboy was elected king; another, prime minister or vizier; another, *kotwal*, or prefect of the police; and others, constables. Every day for several days together they saw the Brahman passing by weeping. One day the cowboy king asked his vizier whether he knew why the Brahman wept every day. On the vizier not being able to answer the question, the cowboy king ordered one of his constables to bring the Brahman to him. One of them went and said to the Brahman—'The king requires your immediate attendance.'

The Brahman replied—'What for? I have just come from the king, and he put me off till to-morrow. Why does he want me again?' 'It is our king that wants you—our neat-herd king,' rejoined the constable. 'Who is neat-herd king?' asked the Brahman. 'Come and see,' was the reply. The neat-herd king then asked the Brahman why he every day went away weeping. The Brahman then told him his sad story. The neat-herd king, after hearing the whole, said, 'I understand your case; I will give you again all your rights. Only go to the king and ask his permission for me to decide your case.' The Brahman went back to the king of the country, and begged his Majesty to send his case to the neat-herd king, who had offered to decide it. The king, whom the case had greatly puzzled, granted the permission sought. The following morning was fixed for the trial. The neat-herd king, who saw through the whole, brought with him next day a phial with a narrow neck. The Brahman and the ghost-Brahman both appeared at the bar. After a great deal of examination of witnesses and of speech-making, the neat-herd king said—'Well, I have heard enough. I'll decide the case at once. Here is this phial. Whichever of you will enter into it shall be declared by the court to be the rightful owner of the house the title of which is in dispute. Now, let me see, which of you will enter.'

The Brahman said—'You are a neat-herd, and your intellect is that of a neat-herd. What man can enter into such a small phial?' 'If you cannot enter,' said the neat-herd king, 'then you are not the rightful owner. What do you say, sir, to this?' turning to the ghost-Brahman and addressing him. 'If you can enter into the phial, then the house and the wife and the mother become yours.' 'Of course I will enter,' said the ghost. And true to his word, to the wonder of all, he made himself into a small creature like an insect, and entered into the phial. The neat-herd king forthwith corked up the phial, and the ghost could not get out. Then, addressing the Brahman, the neat-herd king said, 'Throw this phial into the bottom of the sea, and take possession of your house, wife, and mother.' The Brahman did so, and lived happily for many years and begat sons and daughters.

Here my story endeth,
The Natiya-thorn withereth, etc.

39

The Haughty Princess

(Irish)

There was once a very worthy king, whose daughter was the greatest beauty that could be seen far or near, but she was as proud as Lucifer, and no king or prince would she agree to marry. Her father was tired out at last, and invited every king, and prince, and duke, and earl that he knew or didn't know to come to his court to give her one trial more. They all came, and next day after breakfast they stood in a row in the lawn, and the princess walked along in the front of them to make her choice. One was fat, and says she, 'I won't have you, Beer-barrel!' One was tall and thin, and to him she said, 'I won't have you, Ramrod!' To a white-faced man she said, 'I won't have you, Pale Death', and to a red-cheeked man she said, 'I won't have you, Cockscomb!' She stopped a little before the last of all, for he was a fine man in face and form. She wanted to find some defect in him, but he had nothing remarkable but a ring of brown curling hair under his chin. She admired him a little, and then carried it off with, 'I won't have you, Whiskers!'

So all went away, and the king was so vexed, he said to her, 'Now to punish your *impudence*, I'll give you to the first beggarman or singing *sthronshuch* that calls'; and, as sure as the hearth-money, a fellow all over-rags, and hair that came to his shoulders, and a bushy red beard all over his face, came next morning, and began to sing before the parlour window.

When the song was over, the hall-door was opened, the singer asked in, the priest brought, and the princess married to Beardy. She roared and she bawled, but her father didn't mind her. 'There,' says he to the bridegroom, 'is five guineas for you. Take your wife out of my sight, and never let me lay eyes on you or her again.'

Off he led her, and dismal enough she was. The only thing that gave her relief was the tones of her husband's voice and his genteel manners. 'Whose wood is this?' said she, as they were going through one. 'It belongs to the king you called Whiskers yesterday.' He gave her the same answer about meadows and corn-fields, and at last a fine city. 'Ah, what a fool I was!' said she to herself. 'He was a fine man, and I might have him for a husband.' At last they were coming up to a poor cabin. 'Why are you bringing me here?' says the poor lady. 'This was my house,' said he, 'and now it's yours.' She began to cry, but she was tired and hungry, and she went in with him.

Ovoch! There was neither a table laid out, nor a fire burning, and she was obliged to help her husband to light it, and boil their dinner, and clean up the place after; and next day he made her put on a stuff gown and a cotton handkerchief. When she had her house readied up, and no business to keep her employed, he brought home *sallies*, peeled them, and showed her how to make baskets. But the hard twigs bruised her delicate fingers, and she began to cry. Well, then he asked her to mend their clothes, but the needle drew blood from her fingers, and she cried again. He couldn't bear to see her tears, so he bought a creel of earthenware, and sent her to the market to sell them. This was the hardest trial of all, but she looked so handsome and sorrowful, and had such a nice air about her, that all her pans, and jugs, and plates, and dishes were gone before noon, and the only mark of her old pride she showed was a slap she gave a buckeen across the face when he *axed* her to go in an' take share of a quart.

Well, her husband was so glad, he sent her with another creel the next day; but faith! Her luck was after deserting her. A drunken huntsman came up riding, and his beast got in among her ware, and made *brishe* of every mother's son of 'em. She went home cryin', and her husband wasn't at all pleased. 'I see,' said he, 'you're not fit for business. Come along, I'll get you a kitchen-maid's place in the palace. I know the cook.'

So the poor thing was obliged to stifle her pride once more. She was kept very busy, and the footman and the butler would be very impudent about looking for a kiss, but she let a screech out of her the first attempt was made, and the cook gave the fellow such a lambasting with the besom that he made no second offer. She went home to her husband every night, and she carried broken victuals wrapped in papers in her side pockets.

A week after she got service there was great bustle in the kitchen. The king was going to be married, but no one knew who the bride was to be. Well, in the evening the cook filled the princess's pockets with cold meat and puddings, and, says she, 'Before you go, let us have a look at the great doings in the big parlour.' So they came near the door to get a peep, and who should come out but the king himself, as handsome as you please, and no other but King Whiskers himself. 'Your handsome helper must pay for her peeping,' said he to the cook, 'and dance a jig with me.' Whether she would or no, he held her hand and brought her into the parlour. The fiddlers struck up, and away went *him* with *her*. But they hadn't danced two steps when the meat and the *puddens* flew out of her pockets. Every one roared out, and she flew to the door, crying piteously. But she was soon caught by the king, and taken into the back parlour. 'Don't you know me, my darling?' said he. 'I'm both King Whiskers, your husband the ballad-singer, and the drunken huntsman. Your father knew me well enough when he gave you to me, and all was to drive your pride out of you.' Well, she didn't know how she was with fright, and shame, and joy. Love was uppermost anyhow, for she laid her head on her husband's breast and cried like a child. The maids-of-honour soon had her away and dressed her as fine as hands and pins could do it; and there were her mother and father, too; and while the company were wondering what end of the handsome girl and the king, he and his queen, *who* they didn't know in her fine clothes, and the other king and queen, came in, and such rejoicings and fine doings as there was, none of us will ever see, any way.

40

The Widow's Son

(Subanun)

In a little house at the edge of a village lived a widow with her only son, and they were very happy together. The son was kind to his mother, and they made their living by growing rice in clearings on the mountain side and by hunting wild pig in the forest.

One evening when their supply of meat was low, the boy said:

'Mother, I am going to hunt pig in the morning, and I wish you would prepare rice for me before daylight.'

So the widow rose early and cooked the rice, and at dawn the boy started out with his spear and dog.

Some distance from the village, he entered the thick forest. He walked on and on, ever on the lookout for game, but none appeared. At last when he had traveled far and the sun was hot, he sat down on a rock to rest and took out his brass box to get a piece of betel-nut. He prepared the nut and leaf for chewing, and as he did so he wondered why it was that he had been so unsuccessful that day. But even as he pondered he heard his dog barking sharply, and cramming the betel-nut into his mouth he leaped up and ran toward the dog.

As he drew near he could see that the game was a fine large

pig, all black save its four legs which were white. He lifted his spear and took aim, but before he could throw the pig started to run, and instead of going toward a water course it ran straight up the mountain. The boy went on in hot pursuit, and when the pig paused he again took aim, but before he could throw it ran on.

Six times the pig stopped just long enough for the boy to take aim, and then started on before he could throw. The seventh time, however, it halted on the top of a large flat rock and the boy succeeded in killing it.

He tied its legs together with a piece of rattan and was about to start for home with the pig on his back, when to his surprise a door in the large stone swung open and a man stepped out.

'Why have you killed my master's pig?' asked the man.

'I did not know that this pig belonged to anyone,' replied the widow's son. 'I was hunting, as I often do, and when my dog found the pig I helped him to catch it.'

'Come in and see my master,' said the man, and the boy followed him into the stone where he found himself in a large room. The ceiling and floor were covered with peculiar cloth that had seven wide stripes of red alternating with a like number of yellow stripes. When the master of the place appeared his trousers were of seven colors, as were also his jacket and the kerchief about his head.

The master ordered betel-nut, and when it was brought they chewed together. Then he called for wine, and it was brought in a jar so large that it had to be set on the ground under the house, and even then the top came so high above the floor that they brought a seat for the widow's son, and it raised him just high enough to drink from the reed in the top of the jar.

He drank seven cups of wine, and then they ate rice and fish and talked together.

The master did not blame the boy for killing the pig, and declared that he wished to make a brother of him. So they became friends, and the boy remained seven days in the stone. At the end of that time, he said that he must return to his mother who would be worried about him. In the early morning he left the strange house and started for home.

At first he walked briskly, but as the morning wore on he went more slowly, and finally when the sun was high he sat down on a rock to rest. Suddenly looking up, he saw before him seven men each armed with a spear, a shield, and a sword. They were dressed in different colors, and each man had eyes the same color as his clothes. The leader, who was dressed all in red with red eyes to match, spoke first, asking the boy where he was going. The boy replied that he was going home to his mother who would be looking for him, and added:

'Now I ask where you are going, all armed ready for war.'

'We are warriors,' replied the man in red. 'And we go up and down the world killing whatever we see that has life. Now that we have met you, we must kill you also.'

The boy, startled by this strange speech, was about to answer when he heard a voice near him say: 'Fight, for they will try to kill you,' and upon looking up he saw his spear, shield, and sword which he had left at home. Then he knew that the command came from a spirit, so he took his weapons and began to fight. For three days and nights they contended, and never before had the seven seen one man so brave. On the fourth day the leader was wounded and fell dead, and then, one by one, the other six fell.

When they were all killed, the widow's son was so crazed with fighting that he thought no longer of returning home, but started out to find more to slay.

In his wanderings he came to the home of a great giant whose house was already full of the men he had conquered in battle, and he called up from outside:

'Is the master of the house at home? If he is, let him come out and fight.'

This threw the giant into a rage, and seizing his shield and his spear, the shaft of which was the trunk of a tree, he sprang to the door and leaped to the ground, not waiting to go down the notched pole which served for steps. He looked around for his antagonist, and seeing only the widow's son he roared:

'Where is the man that wants to fight? That thing? It is only a fly!'

The boy did not stop to answer, but rushed at the giant with his knife; and for three days and nights they struggled, till the giant fell, wounded at the waist.

After that the widow's son stopped only long enough to burn the giant's house, and then rushed on looking for someone else to slay. Suddenly he again heard the voice which had bade him fight with the seven men, and this time it said: 'Go home now, for your mother is grieved at your absence.' In a rage he sprang forward with his sword, though he could see no enemy. Then the spirit which had spoken to him made him sleep for a short time. When he awoke the rage was spent.

Again the spirit appeared, and it said: 'The seven men whom you killed were sent to kill you by the spirit of the great stone, for he looked in your hand and saw that you were to marry the orphan girl whom he himself wished to wed. But you have conquered. Your enemies are dead. Go home now and prepare a great quantity of wine, for I shall bring your enemies to life again, and you will all live in peace.'

So the widow's son went home, and his mother, who had believed him dead, was filled with joy at his coming, and all the people in the town came out to welcome him. When he had told them his story, they hastened to get wine, and all day they bore jarsful to the widow's house.

That night there was a great feast, and the spirit of the great stone, his seven warriors, the friendly spirit, and the giant all came. The widow's son married the orphan girl, while another beautiful woman became the wife of the spirit of the stone.

41

How Mushrooms First Grew

(West African)

Long, long ago there dwelt in a town two brothers whose bad habits brought them much trouble. Day by day they got more deeply in debt. Their creditors gave them no peace, so at last they ran away into the woods. They became highway robbers.

But they were not happy. Their minds were troubled by their evil deeds. At last they decided to go home, make a big farm, and pay off their debts gradually.

They accordingly set to work and soon had quite a fine farm prepared for corn. As the soil was good, they hoped the harvest would bring them in much money.

Unfortunately, that very day a bushfowl came along. Being hungry, it scratched up all the newly planted seeds and ate them.

The two poor brothers, on arriving at the field next day, were dismayed to find all their work quite wasted. They put down a trap for the thief. That evening the bushfowl was caught in it. The two brothers, when they came and found the bird, told it that now all their debts would be transferred to it because it had robbed them of the means of paying the debts themselves.

The poor bird—in great trouble at having such a burden thrust upon it—made a nest under a silk-cotton tree. There it began to lay eggs, meaning to hatch them and sell the young birds for money to pay off the debt.

A terrible hurricane came, however, and a branch of the tree came down. All the eggs were smashed. As a result, the bushfowl transferred the debts to the tree, as it had broken the eggs.

The silk-cotton tree was in dismay at having such a big sum of money to pay off. It immediately set to work to make as much silk cotton as it possibly could, that it might sell it.

An elephant, not knowing all that had happened, came along. Seeing the silk cotton, he came to the tree and plucked down all its bearings. By this means the debts were transferred to the poor elephant.

The elephant was very sad when he found what he had done. He wandered away into the desert, thinking of a way to make money. He could think of none.

As he stood quietly under a tree, a poor hunter crept up. This man thought he was very lucky to find such a fine elephant standing so still. He at once shot him.

Just before the animal died, he told the hunter that now the debts would have to be paid by him. The hunter was much grieved when he heard this, as he had no money at all.

He walked home wondering what he could do to make enough money to pay the debts. In the darkness he did not see the stump of a tree which the overseers had cut down in the road. He fell and broke his leg. By this means the debts were transferred to the tree-stump.

Not knowing this, a party of white ants came along next morning and began to eat into the tree. When they had broken it nearly to the ground, the tree told them that now the debts were theirs, as they had killed it.

The ants, being very wise, held a council together to find out how best they could make money. They decided each to contribute as much as possible. With the proceeds one of their young men would go to the nearest market and buy pure linen thread. This they would weave and sell and the profits would go to help pay the debts.

This was done. From time to time all the linen in stock was brought and spread out in the sunshine to keep it in good condition. When men see this linen lying out on the ant-hills, they call it 'mushroom', and gather it for food.

The Demon Cat

(Irish)

There was a woman in Connemara, the wife of a fisherman; as he had always good luck, she had plenty of fish at all times stored away in the house ready for market. But, to her great annoyance, she found that a great cat used to come in at night and devour all the best and finest fish. So she kept a big stick by her, and determined to watch.

One day, as she and a woman were spinning together, the house suddenly became quite dark; and the door was burst open as if by the blast of the tempest, when in walked a huge black cat, who went straight up to the fire, then turned round and growled at them.

'Why, surely this is the devil,' said a young girl, who was by, sorting fish.

'I'll teach you how to call me names,' said the cat; and, jumping at her, he scratched her arm till the blood came. 'There, now,' she said, 'you will be more civil another time when a gentleman comes to see you.' And with that he walked over to the door and shut it close, to prevent any of them going out, for the poor young girl, while crying loudly from fright and pain, had made a desperate rush to get away.

Just then a man was going by, and hearing the cries, he pushed open the door and tried to get in; but the cat stood on the threshold, and would let no one pass. On this the man attacked him with his stick, and gave him a sound blow; the cat, however, was more than a match in the fight, for it flew at him and tore his face and hands so badly that the man at last took to his heels and ran away as fast as he could.

'Now, it's time for my dinner,' said the cat, going up to examine the fish that was laid out on the tables. 'I hope the fish is good to-day. Now, don't disturb me, nor make a fuss; I can help myself.' With that he jumped up, and began to devour all the best fish, while he growled at the woman.

'Away, out of this, you wicked beast,' she cried, giving it a blow with the tongs that would have broken its back, only it was a devil; 'out of this; no fish shall you have to-day.'

But the cat only grinned at her, and went on tearing and spoiling and devouring the fish, evidently not a bit the worse for the blow. On this, both the women attacked it with sticks, and struck hard blows enough to kill it, on which the cat glared at them, and spit fire; then, making a leap, it tore their heads and arms till the blood came, and the frightened women rushed shrieking from the house.

But presently the mistress returned, carrying with her a bottle of holy water; and, looking in, she saw the cat still devouring the fish, and not minding. So she crept over quietly and threw holy water on it without a word. No sooner was this done than a dense black smoke filled the place, through which nothing was seen but the two red eyes of the cat, burning like coals of fire. Then the smoke gradually cleared away, and she saw the body of the creature burning slowly till it became shrivelled and black like a cinder, and finally disappeared. And from that time the fish remained untouched and safe from harm, for the power of the evil one was broken, and the demon cat was seen no more.

43

The Woman Who Had a Bear as a Foster-Son

(Greenland, Eskimo)

There was once an old woman living in a place where others lived. She lived nearest the shore, and when those who lived in houses up above had been out hunting, they gave her both meat and blubber.

And once they were out hunting as usual, and now and again they got a bear, so that they frequently ate bear's meat. And they came home with a whole bear. The old woman received a piece from the ribs as her share, and took it home to her house. After she had come home to her house, the wife of the man who had killed the bear came to the window and said:

'Dear little old woman in there, would you like to have a bear's cub?'

And the old woman went and fetched it, and brought it into her house, shifted her lamp, and placed the cub, because it was frozen, up on to the drying frame to thaw. Suddenly she noticed that it moved a little, and took it down to warm it. Then she roasted some blubber, for she had heard that bears lived on blubber, and in this way she fed it from that time onwards, giving it greaves to eat and melted blubber to drink, and it lay beside her at night.

And after it had begun to lie beside her at night it grew very fast, and she began to talk to it in human speech, and thus it gained the mind of a human being, and when it wished to ask its foster-mother for food, it would sniff.

The old woman now no longer suffered want, and those living near brought her food for the cub. The children came sometimes to play with it, but then the old woman would say:

'Little bear, remember to sheathe your claws when you play with them.'

In the morning, the children would come to the window and call in:

'Little bear, come out and play with us, for now we are going to play.'

And when they went out to play together, it would break the children's toy harpoons to pieces, but whenever it wanted to give any one of the children a push, it would always sheathe its claws. But at last it grew so strong, that it nearly always made the children cry. And when it had grown so strong the grown-up people began to play with it, and they helped the old woman in this way, in making the bear grow stronger. But after a time not even grown men dared play with it, so great was its strength, and then they said to one another:

'Let us take it with us when we go out hunting. It may help us to find seal.'

And so one day in the dawn, they came to the old woman's window and cried:

'Little bear, come and earn a share of our catch; come out hunting with us, bear.'

But before the bear went out, it sniffed at the old woman. And then it went out with the men.

On the way, one of the men said:

'Little bear, you must keep down wind, for if you do not so, the game will scent you, and take fright.'

One day when they had been out hunting and were returning home, they called in to the old woman:

'It was very nearly killed by the hunters from the northward; we hardly managed to save it alive. Give therefore some mark by which it may be known; a broad collar of plaited sinews about its neck.'

And so the old foster-mother made a mark for it to wear; a collar of plaited sinews, as broad as a harpoon line.

And after that it never failed to catch seal, and was stronger even than the strongest of hunters, and never stayed at home even in the worst of all weather. Also it was not bigger than an ordinary bear. All the people in the other villages knew it now, and although they sometimes came near to catching it, they would always let it go as soon as they saw its collar.

But now the people from beyond Angmagssalik heard that there was a bear which could not be caught, and then one of them said:

'If ever I see it, I will kill it.'

But the others said:

'You must not do that; the bear's foster-mother could ill manage without its help. If you see it, do not harm it, but leave it alone, as soon as you see its mark.'

One day when the bear came home as usual from hunting, the old foster-mother said:

'Whenever you meet with men, treat them as if you were of one kin with them; never seek to harm them unless they first attack.'

And it heard the foster-mother's words and did as she had said.

And thus the old foster-mother kept the bear with her. In the summer it went out hunting in the sea, and in winter on the ice, and the other hunters now learned to know its ways, and received shares of its catch.

Once during a storm the bear was away hunting as usual, and did not come home until evening. Then it sniffed at its foster-mother and sprang up on to the bench, where its place was on the southern side. Then the old foster-mother went out of the house, and found outside the body of a dead man, which the bear had hauled home. Then without going in again, the old woman went hurrying to the nearest house, and cried at the window:

'Are you all at home?'

'Why?'

'The little bear has come home with a dead man, one whom I do not know.'

When it grew light, they went out and saw that it was the man from the north, and they could see he had been running fast, for he had drawn off his furs, and was in his underbreeches. Afterwards they heard that it was his comrades who had urged the bear to resistance, because he would not leave it alone.

A long time after this had happened, the old foster-mother said to the bear:

'You had better not stay with me here always; you will be killed if you do, and that would be a pity. You had better leave me.'

And she wept as she said this. But the bear thrust its muzzle right down to the floor and wept, so greatly did it grieve to go away from her.

After this, the foster-mother went out every morning as soon as dawn appeared, to look at the weather, and if there were but a cloud as big as one's hand in the sky, she said nothing.

But one morning when she went out, there was not even a cloud as big as a hand, and so she came in and said:

'Little bear, now you had better go; you have your own kin far away out there.'

But when the bear was ready to set out, the old foster-mother, weeping very much, dipped her hands in oil and smeared them with soot, and stroked the bear's side as it took leave of her, but in such manner that it could not see what she was doing. The bear sniffed at her and went away. But the old foster-mother wept all through that day, and her fellows in the place mourned also for the loss of their bear.

But men say that far to the north, when many bears are abroad, there will sometimes come a bear as big as an iceberg, with a black spot on its side.

44

The First Month

(Japanese)

Little Good Boy had just finished eating the last of five rice cakes called 'dango', that had been strung on a skewer of bamboo and dipped in soy sauce, when he said to his little sister, called Chrysanthemum:—

'O-Kiku, it is soon the great festival of the New Year.'

'What shall we do then?' asked little O-Kiku, not clearly remembering the festival of the previous year.

Thus questioned, Yoshi-san had his desired opening to hold forth on the coming delights, and he replied:—

'Men will come the evening before the great feast-day and help Plum-blossom, our maid, to clean all the house with brush and broom. Others will set up the decoration in front of our honoured gateway. They will dig two small holes and plant a gnarled, black-barked father-pine branch on the left, and the slighter reddish mother-pine branch on the right. They will then put with these the tall knotted stem of a bamboo, with its smooth, hard green leaves that chatter when the wind blows. Next they will take a grass rope, about as long as a tall man, fringed with grass, and decorated with zigzag strips of white paper. These, our noble father says, are meant for rude images of men offering themselves in homage to the august gods.'

'Oh, yes! I have not forgotten,' interrupts Chrysanthemum, 'this cord is stretched from bamboo to bamboo; and Plum-blossom says the rope is to bar out the nasty two-toed, red, gray, and black demons, the badgers, the foxes, and other evil spirits from crossing our threshold. But I think it is the next part of the arch which is the prettiest, the whole bunch of things they tie in the middle of the rope. There is the crooked-back lobster, like a bowed old man, with all around the camellia branches, whose young leaves bud before the old leaves fall. There are pretty fern leaves shooting forth in pairs, and deep down between them the little baby fern-leaf. There is the bitter yellow orange, whose name, you know, means "many parents and children." The name of the black piece of charcoal is a pun on our homestead.'

'But best of all,' says Yoshi-san, 'I like the seaweed hontawara, for it tells me of our brave Queen Jingu Kogo, who, lest the troops should be discouraged, concealed from the army that her husband the king had died, put on armor, and led the great campaign against Korea. Her troops, stationed at the margin of the sea, were in danger of defeat on account of the lack of fodder for their horses; when she ordered this hontawara to be plucked from the shore, and the horses, freshened by their meal of seaweed, rushed victoriously to battle. On the bronzed clasp of our worthy father's tobacco-pouch is, our noble father says, the Queen with her sword and the dear little baby prince, Hachiman, who was born after the campaign, and who is now our Warrior God, guiding our troops to victory, and that spirit on whose head squats a dragon has risen partly from the deep, to present an offering to the Queen and the Prince.'

'Then there is another seaweed, whose name is a pun on "rejoicing". There is the lucky bag that I made, for last year, of a square piece of paper into which we put chestnuts and the roe of a herring and dried persimmon fruit. Then I tied up the paper with red and white paper-string, that the sainted gods might know it was an offering.'

'Bronze fishes sitting on their throats.'

Yoshi-san and his little sister had now reached the great gate ornamented with huge bronze fishes sitting on their throats and twisting aloft their forked tails, that was near their home. He told his sister she must wait to know more about the great festival till the time arrived. They shuffled off their shoes, bowed, till their foreheads touched the ground, to their parents, ate their evening bowl of rice and salt fish, said a prayer and burnt a stick of incense to many-armed Buddha at the family altar. They spread their cotton-wadded quilts, rested their dear little shaved heads, with quaint circlet of hair, on the roll of cotton covered with white paper that formed the cushion of their hard wooden pillows. Soon they fell asleep to their mother's monotonously chanted lullaby of 'Nenné ko'.

'Sleep, my child, sleep, my child,
Where is thy nurse gone?
She is gone to the mountains
To buy thee sweetmeats.
What shall she buy thee?
The thundering drum, the bamboo pipe,
The trundling man, or the paper kite.'

The great festival drew still nearer, to the children's delight, as they watched the previously described graceful bamboo arch rise before their gateposts. Then came a party of three with an oven, a bottomless tub, and some matting to replace the bottom. They shifted the pole that carried these utensils from their shoulders, and commenced to make the Japanese cake that may be viewed as the equivalent of a Christmas pudding. They mixed a paste of rice and put the sticky mass, to prevent rebounding, on the soft mat in the tub. The third man then beat for a long time the rice cake with a heavy mallet. Yoshi-san liked to watch the strong man swing down his mallet with dull resounding thuds. The well-beaten dough was then made up into flattish rounds of varying size on a pastry board one of the men had brought. Three cakes of graduated size formed a pyramid that was placed conspicuously on a lacquered stand, and the cakes were only to be eaten on the 11th of January.

The mother told Plum-blossom and the children to get their clogs and overcoats and hoods, for she was going to get the New Year's decorations. The party shuffled off till they came to a stall where were big grass ropes and fringes and quaint grass boats filled with supposed bales of merchandise in straw coverings, a sun in red paper, and at bow and stern sprigs of fir. The whole was brightened by bits of gold leaf, lightly stuck on, that quivered here and there. When the children had chosen the harvest ship that seemed most besprinkled with gold, Plum-blossom bargained about the price. The mother, as a matter of form and rank, had pretended to take no interest in the purchase. She took her purse out of her sash, handed it to her servant, who opened it, paid the shopman, and then returned the purse to her mistress. This she did with the usual civility of first raising it to her forehead. The decorations they hung up in their sitting-room. Then they sent presents, such as large dried carp, tea, eggs, shoes, kerchiefs, fruits, sweets, or toys to various friends and dependants.

On the 1st of January all were early astir, for the father, dressed at dawn in full European evening dress, as is customary on such occasions, had to pay his respects at the levee of the Emperor. When this duty was over, he returned home and received visitors of rank inferior to himself. Later in the day and on the following day he paid visits of New Year greeting to all his friends. He took a present to those to whom he had sent no gift. Sometimes he had his little boy with him. For these visits Yoshi-san, in place of his usual flowing robe, loose trousers, and sash, wore a funny little knickerbocker suit, felt hat, and boots. These latter, though he thought them grand, felt very uncomfortable after his straw sandals. They were more troublesome to take off before stepping on the straw mats, that, being used as chairs as well as carpets, it would be a rudeness to soil. The maids, always kneeling, presented them with tiny cups of tea on oval saucers, which, remaining in the maid's hand, served rather as waiters. Sweetmeats, too, usually of a soft, sticky nature, but sometimes hard like sugar-plums, and called 'fire-sweets', were offered on carved lotus-leaf or lacquered trays.

For the 2nd of January Plum-blossom bought some pictures of the treasure-ship or ship of riches, in which were seated the seven Gods of Wealth. It has been sung thus about this Ship of Luck:—

'Nagaki yo no,	It is a long night.
To no numuri no.	The gods of luck sleep.
Mina mé samé.	They all open their eyes.
Nami nori funé no.	They ride in a boat on the waves.
Oto no yoki kana.'	The sound is pleasing!

These pictures they each tied on their pillow to bring lucky dreams. Great was the laughter in the morning when they related their dreams. Yoshi-san said he had dreamt he had a beautiful portmanteau full of nice foreign things, such as comforters, note-books, pencils, india-rubber, condensed milk, lama, wide-awakes, boots, and brass jewellery. Just as he opened it, everything vanished and he found only a torn fan, an odd chop-stick, a horse's cast straw shoe, and a live crow.

When at home, the children, for the first few days of the New Year, dressed in their best crepe, made up in three silken-wadded layers. Their crest was embroidered on the centre of the back and on the sleeves of the quaintly flowered long upper skirt. Beneath its wadded hem peeped the scarlet rolls of the hems of their under-dresses, and then the white-stockinged feet, with, passing between the toes, the scarlet thong of the black-lacquered clog. The little girl's sash was of many-flowered brocade, with scarlet broidered pouch hanging at her right side. A scarlet over-sash kept the large sash-knot in its place. Her hair was gay with knot of scarlet crinkled crepe, lacquered comb, and hairpin of tiny golden battledore. Resting thereon were a shuttlecock of coral, another pin of a tiny red lobster and a green pine sprig made of silk. In her belt was coquettishly stuck the butterfly-broidered case that held her quire of paper pocket-handkerchiefs. The brother's dress was of a simpler style and soberer coloring. His pouch of purple had a dragon worked on it, and the hair of his partly shaven head was tied into a little gummed tail with white paper-string. They spent most of the day playing with their pretty new battledores, striking with its plain side the airy little shuttlecock whose head is made of a black seed. All the while they sang a rhyme on the numbers up to ten:—

'Hitogo ni futa-go—mi-watashi yo me-go,
Itsu yoni musashi nan no yakushi,
Kokono-ya ja—to yo.'

When tired of this fun, they would play with a ball made of paper and wadding evenly wound about with thread or silk of various colors. They sang to the throws a song which seems abrupt because some portions have probably fallen into disuse; it runs thus:—

'See opposite—see Shin-kawa! A very beautiful lady who is one of the daughters of a chief magistrate of Odawara-cho. She was married to a salt merchant. He was a man fond of display, and he thought how he would dress her this year. He said to the dyer, "Please dye this brocade and the brocade for the middle dress into seven-or eight-fold dresses"; and the dyer said, "I am a dyer, and therefore I will dye and stretch it. What pattern do you wish?" The merchant replied, "The pattern of falling snow and broken twigs, and in the centre the curved bridge of Gojo."'

Then to fill up the rhyme come the words, 'Chokin, chokera, kokin, kokera,' and the tale goes on: 'Crossing this bridge the girl was struck here and there, and the tea-house girls laughed. Put out of countenance by this ridicule, she drowned herself in the river Karas, the body sunk, the hair floated. How full of grief the husband's heart—now the ball counts a hundred.'

This they varied with another song:—

'One, two, three, four,
Grate hard charcoal, shave kiri wood;
Put in the pocket, the pocket is wet,
Kiyomadzu, on three yenoki trees

Were three sparrows, chased by a pigeon.
The sparrows said, "Chiu, chiu,"
The pigeon said, "po, po,"—now the
Ball counts a hundred.'

The pocket referred to means the bottom of the long sleeve, which is apt to trail and get wet when a child stoops at play. Kiyomadzu may mean a famous temple that bears that name. Sometimes they would simply count the turns and make a sort of game of forfeiting and returning the number of rebounds kept up by each.

Yoshi-san had begun to think battledore and balls too girlish an amusement. He preferred flying his eagle or mask-like kite, or playing at cards, verses, or lotteries. Sometimes he played a lively game with his father, in which the board is divided into squares and diagonals. On these move sixteen men held by one player and one large piece held by the second player. The point of the game is either that the holder of the sixteen pieces hedges the large piece so it that can make no move, or that the big piece takes all its adversaries. A take can only be made by the large piece when it finds a piece immediately on each side of it and a blank point beyond. Or he watched a party of several, with the pictured sheet of Japanese backgammon before them, write their names on slips of paper or wood, and throw in turn a die. The slips are placed on the pictures whose numbers correspond with the throw. At the next round, if the number thrown by the particular player is written on the picture, he finds directions as to which picture to move his slip backward or forward to. He may, however, find his throw a blank and have to remain at his place. The winning consists in reaching a certain picture. When tired of these quieter games, the strolling woman player on a guitar-like instrument, would be called in. Or, a party of Kangura boy performers afforded pastime by the quaint animal-like movements of the draped figure. He wears a huge grotesque scarlet mask on his head, and at times makes this monster appear to stretch out and draw in its neck by an unseen change in position of the mask from the head to the gradually extended and draped hand of the actor. The beat of a drum and the whistle of a bamboo flute formed the accompaniment to the dumb-show acting.

Yoshi-san thought the 4th and 5th days of January great fun, because loud shoutings were heard. Running in the direction of the sound, he found the men of a fire-brigade who had formed a procession to carry their new paper standard, bamboo ladders, paper lanterns, etc. This procession paused at intervals. Then the men steadied the ladder with their long fire-hooks, whilst an agile member of the band mounted the erect ladder and performed gymnastics at the top. His performance concluded, he dismounted, and the march continued, the men as before yelling joyously, at the highest pitch of their voices.

After about a week of fun, life at the villa, gradually resumed its usual course, the father returned to his office, the mother to her domestic employments, and the children to school, all having said for that new year their last joy-wishing greeting— omédéto (congratulations).

45

The Man Who Met Misery

(Czech)

Once upon a time there lived a rich man, so rich that you might almost say he oozed gold. He had a son, and from his boyhood the lad was a real spendthrift, for he knew nothing about hard times. Yet he had often been told that there was Misery in the world. So when he was grown up, he thought: 'Well, I'm sick of staying at home, so I'll go out into the world to see if I can meet Misery.'

He told this to his father, and his father said at once: 'Yes, you can go. If you stay at home, you'll soon turn into a lazy old woman. You'll get experience in the world, and that can't do you any harm.'

So our Francis—that was his name, though really it doesn't matter very much what his name was—took everything he wanted and started off on his travels. So long as he had enough money, he was all right, he couldn't meet with Misery. But when his money was all spent—that's when everybody feels the pinch—he began to hang his head and his travels lost a good deal of their charm. But he told people his name and his father's name, and for a time they helped him. But at last he came into a country that was quite strange to him. There was a vast desert, through which he walked for a long time, and he began to feel hungry and thirsty, but there was no water—no, not so much as would moisten his tongue.

Now, as he went on his way, he saw a flight of stairs going down into a hole, and, without hesitating, down he went.

He came into a cellar, and there he saw a man lying on a table. It was an awfully big man, of the kind that used to be called ogres, and he was snoring like a circular saw.

Francis looked about him, and he saw all sorts of human bones lying about. He thought: 'That's a nice mess. I expect the fellow's a man-eater, and he'll swallow me down like a currant. I'm done for now.'

He would have liked to go away, but he was afraid to move. But he had a dagger, so he drew it from its sheath without making any noise, and tried to steal up to the ogre quietly. The ogre's head was lying on the table, so he pierced both his eyes with the dagger. The ogre sprang up, cursing horribly. He groped about him and found that he was totally blind.

Francis cleared the stairs in two jumps and off he ran, trying to get as far from the ogre as he could. But the ogre knew the place well and kept close on his heels.

'To think that a shrimp like that could make me suffer so!' he thought; and yet he found that, run as he would, he couldn't catch the lad. So he cried out: 'Wait a bit, you worm! Since you're such a champion and have managed to tackle me, I'll give you something to remember me by.'

As he said this, he flung a ring at the lad, and the jewel in it shone like flame. The lad heard the ring tinkle as he ran by, so he picked it up and put it on his finger. But as soon as the ring was on his finger, the giant called out: 'Where are you, ring?' And the ring answered: 'Here I am,' and the ogre ran after the sound. Francis jumped on one side, but the ogre called out again, 'Where are you?' and the ring answered: 'Here!'

So it went on for some time, until Francis was so tired that his only thought was: 'Well, if he kills me, he kills me.' He tried to pull the ring off, but it clung tight, really cutting into the flesh, and the ogre was still following close on his heels. At last—there was no other choice, for the ring kept on calling out 'Here I am'—Francis stretched out that finger, and the ogre broke it off with one grip. Off ran Francis, glad enough to get off with his life.

When he reached home, they asked him: 'Did you meet Misery?'

'Indeed I did. I know what it is now. It gave me a nice run for it. It's an awful thing, and there's no joking with it.'

46

The Origin of the Narran Lake

(Australian)

Old Byamee said to his two young wives, Birrahgnooloo and Cunnunbeillee, 'I have stuck a white feather between the hind legs of a bee, and am going to let it go and then follow it to its nest, that I may get honey. While I go for the honey, go you two out and get frogs and yams, then meet me at Coorigel Spring, where we will camp, for sweet and clear is the water there.' The wives, taking their goolays and yam sticks, went out as he told them. Having gone far, and dug out many yams and frogs, they were tired when they reached Coorigel, and, seeing the cool, fresh water, they longed to bathe. But first they built a bough shade, and there left their goolays holding their food, and the yams and frogs they had found. When their camp was ready for the coming of Byamee, who having wooed his wives with a nullah-nullah, kept them obedient by fear of the same weapon, then went the girls to the spring to bathe. Gladly they plunged in, having first divested themselves of their goomillahs, which they were still young enough to wear, and which they left on the ground near the spring. Scarcely were they enjoying the cool rest the water gave their hot, tired limbs, when they were seized and swallowed by two kurreahs. Having swallowed the girls, the kurreahs dived into an opening in the side of the spring, which was the entrance to an underground watercourse leading to the Narran River. Through this passage they went, taking all the water from the spring with them into the Narran, whose course they also dried as they went along.

Meantime Byamee, unwitting the fate of his wives, was honey hunting. He had followed the bee with the white feather on it for some distance; then the bee flew on to some budtha flowers, and would move no further. Byamee said, 'Something has happened, or the bee would not stay here and refuse to be moved on towards its nest. I must go to Coorigel Spring and see if my wives are safe. Something terrible has surely happened.' And Byamee turned in haste towards the spring. When he reached there he saw the bough shed his wives had made, he saw the yams they had dug from the ground, and he saw the frogs, but Birrahgnooloo and Cunnunbeillee he saw not. He called aloud for them. But no answer. He went towards the spring; on the edge of it he saw the goomillahs of his wives. He looked into the spring and, seeing it dry, he said, 'It is the work of the kurreahs; they have opened the underground passage and gone with my wives to the river, and opening the passage has dried the spring. Well do I know where the passage joins the Narran, and there will I swiftly go.' Arming himself with spears and woggarahs he started in pursuit. He soon reached the deep hole where the underground channel of the Coorigel joined the Narran. There he saw what he had never seen before, namely, this deep hole dry. And he said: 'They have emptied the holes as they went along, taking the water with them. But well know I the deep holes of the river. I will not follow the bend, thus trebling the distance I have to go, but I will cut across from big hole to big hole, and by so doing I may yet get ahead of the kurreahs.' On swiftly sped Byamee, making short cuts from big hole to big hole, and his track is still marked by the morilla ridges that stretch down the Narran, pointing in towards the deep holes. Every hole as he came to it he found dry, until at last he reached the end of the Narran; the hole there was still quite wet and muddy, then he knew he was near his enemies, and soon he saw them. He managed to get, unseen, a little way ahead of the kurreahs. He hid himself behind a big dheal tree. As the kurreahs came near they separated, one turning to go in another direction. Quickly Byamee hurled one spear after another, wounding both kurreahs, who writhed with pain and lashed their tails furiously, making great hollows in the ground, which the water they had brought with them quickly filled. Thinking they might again escape him, Byamee drove them from the water with his spears, and then, at close quarters, he killed them with his woggarahs. And ever afterwards at flood time, the Narran flowed into this hollow which the kurreahs in their writhings had made.

When Byamee saw that the kurreahs were quite dead, he cut them open and took out the bodies of his wives. They were covered with wet slime, and seemed quite lifeless; but he carried them and laid them on two nests of red ants. Then he sat down at some little distance and watched them. The ants quickly covered the bodies, cleaned them rapidly of the wet slime, and soon Byamee noticed the muscles of the girls twitching. 'Ah,' he said, 'there is life, they feel the sting of the ants.'

Almost as he spoke came a sound as of a thunder-clap, but the sound seemed to come from the ears of the girls. And as the echo was dying away, slowly the girls rose to their feet.

For a moment they stood apart, a dazed expression on their faces. Then they clung together, shaking as if stricken with a deadly fear. But Byamee came to them and explained how they had been rescued from the kurreahs by him. He bade them to beware of ever bathing in the deep holes of the Narran, lest such holes be the haunt of kurreahs.

Then he bade them look at the water now at Boogira, and he said:

'Soon will the black swans find their way here, the pelicans and the ducks; where there was dry land and stones in the past, in the future there will be water and water-fowl, from henceforth; when the Narran runs it will run into this hole, and by the spreading of its waters will a big lake be made.' And what Byamee said has come to pass, as the Narran Lake shows, with its large sheet of water, spreading for miles, the home of thousands of wild fowl.

47

The Little House

(French)

There was once a man named Prudent, who was a widower and he lived alone with his little daughter. His wife had died a few days after the birth of this little girl, who was named Rosalie.

Rosalie's father had a large fortune. He lived in a great house, which belonged to him. This house was surrounded by a large garden in which Rosalie walked whenever she pleased to do so.

She had been trained with great tenderness and gentleness but her father had accustomed her to the most unquestioning obedience. He forbade her positively to ask him any useless questions or to insist upon knowing anything he did not wish to tell her. In this way, by unceasing care and watchfulness, he had almost succeeded in curing one of Rosalie's great faults, a fault indeed unfortunately too common—curiosity.

Rosalie never left the park, which was surrounded by high walls. She never saw any one but her father. They had no domestic in the house; everything seemed to be done of itself. She always had what she wanted—clothing, books, work, and playthings. Her father educated her himself and although she was nearly fifteen years old, she was never weary and never thought that she might live otherwise and might see more of the world.

There was a little house at the end of the park without windows and with but one door, which was always locked. Rosalie's father entered this house every day and always carried the key about his person. Rosalie thought it was only a little hut in which the garden-tools were kept. She never thought of speaking about it but one day, when she was seeking a watering-pot for her flowers, she said to him:—

'Father, please give me the key of the little house in the garden.'

'What do you want with this key, Rosalie?'

'I want a watering-pot and I think I could find one in that little house.'

'No, Rosalie, there is no watering-pot there.'

Prudent's voice trembled so in pronouncing these words that Rosalie looked up with surprise, and saw that his face was pale and his forehead bathed in perspiration.

'What is the matter, father?' said she, alarmed.

'Nothing, daughter, nothing.'

'It was my asking for the key which agitated you so violently, father. What does this little house contain which frightens you so much?'

'Rosalie, Rosalie! you do not know what you are saying. Go and look for your watering-pot in the green-house.'

'But, father, what is there in the little garden-house?'

'Nothing that can interest you, Rosalie.'

'But why do you go there every day without permitting me to go with you?'

'Rosalie, you know that I do not like to be questioned and that curiosity is the greatest defect in your character.'

Rosalie said no more but she remained very thoughtful. This little house, of which she had never before thought, was now constantly in her mind.

'What can be concealed there?' she said to herself. 'How pale my father turned when I asked his permission to enter! I am sure he thought I should be in some sort of danger. But why does he go there himself every day? It is no doubt to carry food to some ferocious beast confined there. But if it was some wild animal, would I not hear it roar or howl or shake the house? No, I have never heard any sound from this cabin. It cannot then be a beast. Besides, if it was a ferocious beast, it would devour my father when he entered alone. Perhaps, however, it is chained. But if it is indeed chained, then there would be no danger for me. What can it be? A prisoner? My father is good, he would not deprive any unfortunate innocent of light and liberty. Well, I absolutely must discover this mystery. How shall I manage it? If I could only secretly get the key from my father for a half hour! Perhaps some day he will forget it.'

Rosalie was aroused from this chain of reflection by her father, who called to her with a strangely agitated voice.

'Here, father—I am coming.'

She entered the house and looked steadily at her father. His pale, sad countenance indicated great agitation.

More than ever curious, she resolved to feign gaiety and indifference in order to allay her father's suspicions and make him feel secure. In this way she thought she might perhaps obtain possession of the key at some future time. He might not always think of it if she herself seemed to have forgotten it.

They seated themselves at the table. Prudent ate but little

and was sad and silent, in spite of his efforts to appear gay. Rosalie, however, seemed so thoughtless and bright that her father at last recovered his accustomed good spirits.

Rosalie would be fifteen years old in three weeks. Her father had promised an agreeable surprise for this event. A few days passed peacefully away. There remained but fifteen days before her birth-day. One morning Prudent said to Rosalie:—

'My dear child, I am compelled to be absent for one hour. I must go out to arrange something for your birth-day. Wait for me in the house, my dear. Do not yield yourself up to idle curiosity. In fifteen days you will know all that you desire to know, for I read your thoughts and I know what occupies your mind. Adieu, my daughter, beware of curiosity!'

Prudent embraced his daughter tenderly and withdrew, leaving her with great reluctance.

As soon as he was out of sight, Rosalie ran to her father's room and what was her joy to see the key forgotten upon the table! She seized it and ran quickly to the end of the park. Arrived at the little house, she remembered the words of her father, 'Beware of curiosity!' She hesitated, and was upon the point of returning the key without having looked at the house, when she thought she heard a light groan. She put her ear against the door and heard a very little voice singing softly:—

'A lonely prisoner I pine,
No hope of freedom now is mine;
I soon must draw my latest breath,
And in this dungeon meet my death.'

'No doubt,' said Rosalie to herself, 'this is some unfortunate creature whom my father holds captive.'

Tapping softly upon the door, she said: 'Who are you, and what can I do for you?'

'Open the door, Rosalie! I pray you open the door!'

'But why are you a prisoner? Have you not committed some crime?'

'Alas! No, Rosalie. An enchanter keeps me here a prisoner. Save me and I will prove my gratitude by telling you truly who I am.'

Rosalie no longer hesitated: her curiosity was stronger than her obedience. She put the key in the lock, but her hand trembled so that she could not open it. She was about to give up the effort, when the little voice continued:—

'Rosalie, that which I have to tell you will teach you many things which will interest you. Your father is not what he appears to be.'

At these words Rosalie made a last effort, the key turned and the door opened.

48

The Legend of the Wooden Shoe

(Dutch)

In years long gone, too many for the almanac to tell of, or for clocks and watches to measure, millions of good fairies came down from the sun and went into the earth. There, they changed themselves into roots and leaves, and became trees. There were many kinds of these, as they covered the earth, but the pine and birch, ash and oak, were the chief ones that made Holland. The fairies that lived in the trees bore the name of Moss Maidens, or Tree 'Trintjes,' which is the Dutch pet name for Kate, or Katharine.

The oak was the favourite tree, for people lived then on acorns, which they ate roasted, boiled or mashed, or made into meal, from which something like bread was kneaded and baked. With oak bark, men tanned hides and made leather, and, from its timber, boats and houses. Under its branches, near the trunk, people laid their sick, hoping for help from the gods. Beneath the oak boughs, also, warriors took oaths to be faithful to their lords, women made promises, or wives joined hand in hand around its girth, hoping to have beautiful children. Up among its leafy branches the new babies lay, before they were found in the cradle by the other children. To make a young child grow up to be strong and healthy, mothers drew them through a split sapling or young tree. Even more wonderful, as medicine for the country itself, the oak had power to heal. The new land sometimes suffered from disease called the *val* (or fall). When sick with the val, the ground sunk. Then people, houses, churches, barns and cattle all went down, out of sight, and were lost forever, in a flood of water.

But the oak, with its mighty roots, held the soil firm. Stories of dead cities, that had tumbled beneath the waves, and of the famous Forest of Reeds, covering a hundred villages, which disappeared in one night, were known only too well.

Under the birch tree, lovers met to plight their vows, and on its smooth bark was often cut the figure of two hearts joined in one. In summer, the forest furnished shade, and in winter warmth from the fire. In the spring time, the new leaves were a wonder, and in autumn the pigs grew fat on the mast, or the acorns, that had dropped on the ground.

So, for thousands of years, when men made their home in the forest, and wanted nothing else, the trees were sacred.

But by and by, when cows came into the land and sheep and horses multiplied, more open ground was needed for pasture, grain fields and meadows. Fruit trees, bearing apples and pears, peaches and cherries, were planted, and grass, wheat, rye and barley were grown. Then, instead of the dark woods, men liked to have their gardens and orchards open to the sunlight. Still, the people were very rude, and all they had on their bare feet were rough bits of hard leather, tied on through their toes; though most of them went barefooted.

The forests had to be cut down. Men were so busy with the axe, that in a few years, the Wood Land was gone. Then the new 'Holland', with its people and red roofed houses, with its chimneys and windmills, and dykes and storks, took the place of the old Holt Land of many trees.

Now there was a good man, a carpenter and very skilful with his tools, who so loved the oak that he gave himself, and his children after him, the name of Eyck, which is pronounced Ike, and is Dutch for oak. When, before his neighbours and friends, according to the beautiful Dutch custom, he called his youngest born child, to lay the corner-stone of his new house, he bestowed upon her, before them all, the name of Neeltje (or Nellie) Van Eyck.

The carpenter daddy continued to mourn over the loss of the forests. He even shed tears, fearing lest, by and by, there should not one oak tree be left in the country. Moreover, he was frightened at the thought that the new land, made by pushing back the ocean and building dykes, might sink down again and go back to the fishes. In such a case, all the people, the babies and their mothers, men, women, horses and cattle, would be drowned. The Dutch folks were a little too fast, he thought, in winning their acres from the sea.

One day, while sitting on his door-step, brooding sorrowfully, a Moss Maiden and a Tree Elf appeared, skipping along, hand in hand. They came up to him and told him that his ancestral oak had a message for him. Then they laughed and ran away. Van Eyck, which was now the man's full family name, went into the forest and stood under the grand old oak tree, which his fathers loved, and which he would allow none to cut down.

Looking up, the leaves of the tree rustled, and one big branch seemed to sweep near him. Then it whispered in his ear:

'Do not mourn, for your descendants, even many generations hence, shall see greater things than you have witnessed. I and my fellow oak trees shall pass away, but the sunshine shall be spread over the land and make it dry. Then, instead of its falling down, like acorns from the trees, more and better food shall come up from out of the earth. Where green fields now spread, and the cities grow where forests were, we shall come to life again, but in another form. When most needed, we shall furnish you and your children and children's children, with warmth, comfort, fire, light and wealth. Nor need you fear for the land, that it will fall; for, even while living, we, and all the oak trees that are left, and all the birch, beech, and pine trees shall stand on our heads for you. We shall hold up your houses, lest they fall into the ooze and you shall walk and run over our heads. As truly as when rooted in the soil, will we do this. Believe what we tell you, and be happy. We shall turn ourselves upside down for you.'

'I cannot see how all these things can be,' said Van Eyck.

'Fear not, my promise will endure.'

The leaves of the branch rustled for another moment. Then, all was still, until the Moss Maiden and Trintje, the Tree Elf, again, hand in hand, as they tripped along merrily, appeared to him.

'We shall help you and get our friends, the elves, to do the same. Now, do you take some oak wood and saw off two pieces, each a foot long. See that they are well dried. Then set them on the kitchen table to-night, when you go to bed.' After saying this, and looking at each other and laughing, just as girls do, they disappeared.

Pondering on what all this might mean, Van Eyck went to his wood-shed and sawed off the oak timber. At night, after his wife had cleared off the supper table, he laid the foot-long pieces in their place.

When Van Eyck woke up in the morning, he recalled his dream, and, before he was dressed, hurried to the kitchen. There, on the table, lay a pair of neatly made wooden shoes. Not a sign of tools, or shavings could be seen, but the clean wood and pleasant odor made him glad. When he glanced again at the wooden shoes, he found them perfectly smooth, both inside and out. They had heels at the bottom and were nicely pointed at the toes, and, altogether, were very inviting to the foot. He tried them on, and found that they fitted him exactly. He tried to walk on the kitchen floor, which his wife kept scrubbed and polished, and then sprinkled with clean white sand, with broomstick ripples scored in the layers, but for Van Eyck it was like walking on ice. After slipping and balancing himself, as if on a tight rope, and nearly breaking his nose against the wall, he took off the wooden shoes, and kept them off, while inside the house. However, when he went outdoors, he found his new shoes very light, pleasant to the feet and easy to walk in. It was not so much like trying to skate, as it had been in the kitchen.

At night, in his dreams, he saw two elves come through the window into the kitchen. One, a kabouter, dark and ugly, had a box of tools. The other, a light-faced elf, seemed to be the guide. The kabouter at once got out his saw, hatchet, auger, long, chisel-like knife, and smoothing plane. At first, the two elves seemed to be quarrelling, as to who should be boss. Then they settled down quietly to work. The kabouter took the wood and shaped it on the outside. Then he hollowed out, from inside of it, a pair of shoes, which the elf smoothed and polished. Then one elf put his little feet in them and tried to dance, but he only slipped on the smooth floor and flattened his nose; but the other fellow pulled the nose straight again, so it was all right.

They waltzed together upon the wooden shoes, then took them off, jumped out the window, and ran away.

When Van Eyck put the wooden shoes on, he found that out in the fields, in the mud, and on the soft soil, and in sloppy places, this sort of foot gear was just the thing. They did not sink in the mud and the man's feet were comfortable, even after hours of labour. They did not 'draw' his feet, and they kept out the water far better than leather possibly could.

When the Van Eyck vrouw and the children saw how happy Daddy was, they each one wanted a pair. Then they asked him what he called them.

'Klompen,' said he, in good Dutch, and klompen, or klomps, they are to this day.

'I'll make a fortune out of this,' said Van Eyck. 'I'll set up a klomp-winkel (shop for wooden shoes) at once.'

So, going out to the blacksmith's shop, in the village, he had the man who pounded iron fashion for him on his anvil, a set of tools, exactly like those used by the kabouter and the elf, which he had seen in his dream. Then he hung out a sign, marked 'Wooden blocks for shoes.' He made klomps for the little folks just out of the nursery, for boys and girls, for grown men and women, and for all who walked out-of-doors, in the street or on the fields.

Soon klomps came to be the fashion in all the country places. It was good manners, when you went into a house, to take off your wooden shoes and leave them at the door. Even in the towns and cities, ladies wore wooden slippers, especially when walking or working in the garden.

Klomps also set the fashion for soft, warm socks, and stockings made from sheep's wool. Soon, a thousand needles were clicking, to put a soft cushion between one's soles and toes and the wood. Women knitted, even while they walked to market, or gossiped on the streets. The klomp-winkels, or shops of the shoe carpenters, were seen in every village.

When rich beyond his day-dreams, Van Eyck had another joyful night vision. The next day, he wore a smiling countenance. Everybody, who met him on the street, saluted him and asked, in a neighbourly way:

'Good-morning, Mynheer Bly-moe-dig (Mr Cheerful). How do you sail to-day?'

That's the way the Dutch talk—not 'how do you do', but, in their watery country, it is this, 'How do you sail?' or else, 'Hoe gat het u al?' (How goes it with you, already?)

Then Van Eyck told his dream. It was this: The Moss Maiden and Trintje, the wood elf, came to him again at night and danced. They were lively and happy.

'What now?' asked the dreamer, smilingly, of his two visitors.

He had hardly got the question out of his mouth, when in walked a kabouter, all smutty with blacksmith work. In one hand, he grasped his tool box. In the other, he held a curious looking machine. It was a big lump of iron, set in a frame, with ropes to pull it up and let it fall down with a thump.

'What is it?' asked Van Eyck.

'It's a Hey' (a pile driver), said the kabouter, showing him how to use it. 'When men say to you, on the street, to-morrow, "How do you sail?" laugh at them,' said the Moss Maiden, herself laughing.

'Yes, and now you can tell the people how to build cities, with mighty churches with lofty towers, and with high houses like those in other lands. Take the trees, trim the branches off, sharpen the tops, turn them upside down and pound them deep in the ground. Did not the ancient oak promise that the trees would be turned upside down for you? Did they not say you could walk on top of them?'

By this time, Van Eyck had asked so many questions, and kept the elves so long, that the Moss Maiden peeped anxiously through the window. Seeing the day breaking, she and Trintje and the kabouter flew away, so as not to be petrified by the sunrise.

'I'll make another fortune out of this, also,' said the happy man, who, next morning, was saluted as Mynheer Blyd-schap (Mr Joyful).

At once, Van Eyck set up a factory for making pile drivers. Sending men into the woods, who chose the tall, straight trees, he had their branches cut off. Then he sharpened the trunks at one end, and these were driven, by the pile driver, down, far and deep, into the ground. So a foundation, as good as stone, was made in the soft and spongy soil, and well built houses uprose by the thousands. Even the lofty walls of churches stood firm. The spires were unshaken in the storm.

Old Holland had not fertile soil like France, or vast flocks of sheep, producing wool, like England, or armies of weavers, as in the Belgic lands. Yet, soon there rose large cities, with splendid mansions and town halls. As high towards heaven as the cathedrals and towers in other lands, which had rock for foundation, her brick churches rose in the air. On top of the forest trees, driven deep into the sand and clay, dams and dykes were built, that kept out the ocean. So, instead of the old two thousand square miles, there were, in the realm, in the course of years, twelve thousand, rich in green fields and cattle. Then, for all the boys and girls that travel in this land of quaint customs, Holland was a delight.

49

Why Dogs Wag Their Tails

(Visayan)

A rich man in a certain town once owned a dog and a cat, both of which were very useful to him. The dog had served his master for many years and had become so old that he had lost his teeth and was unable to fight any more, but he was a good guide and companion to the cat who was strong and cunning.

The master had a daughter who was attending school at a convent some distance from home, and very often he sent the dog and the cat with presents to the girl.

One day he called the faithful animals and bade them carry a magic ring to his daughter.

'You are strong and brave,' he said to the cat, 'You may carry the ring, but you must be careful not to drop it.'

And to the dog he said: 'You must accompany the cat to guide her and keep her from harm.'

They promised to do their best, and started out. All went well until they came to a river. As there was neither bridge nor boat, there was no way to cross but to swim.

'Let me take the magic ring,' said the dog as they were about to plunge into the water.

'Oh, no,' replied the cat, 'the master gave it to me to carry.'

'But you cannot swim well,' argued the dog. 'I am strong and can take good care of it.'

But the cat refused to give up the ring until finally the dog threatened to kill her, and then she reluctantly gave it to him.

The river was wide and the water so swift that they grew very tired, and just before they reached the opposite bank the dog dropped the ring. They searched carefully, but could not find it anywhere, and after a while they turned back to tell their master of the sad loss. Just before reaching the house, however, the dog was so overcome with fear that he turned and ran away and never was seen again.

The cat went on alone, and when the master saw her coming he called out to know why she had returned so soon and what had become of her companion. The poor cat was frightened, but as well as she could she explained how the ring had been lost and how the dog had run away.

On hearing her story the master was very angry, and commanded that all his people should search for the dog, and that it should be punished by having its tail cut off.

He also ordered that all the dogs in the world should join in the search, and ever since when one dog meets another he says: 'Are you the old dog that lost the magic ring? If so, your tail must be cut off.' Then immediately each shows his teeth and wags his tail to prove that he is not the guilty one.

Since then, too, cats have been afraid of water and will not swim across a river if they can avoid it.

50

The Watchful Servant

(Spanish)

There was once a prince who was going to visit his ladylove, the only daughter of a neighbouring king; and as he required the services of an attendant, he sent for his barber, who was known in the town for his very good behaviour, as well as for his eccentric ways.

'Pablo,' said the prince, 'I want you to go with me to Granada to assist me on my journey. I will reward you handsomely, and you shall lack for nothing in the way of food. But you must don my livery, salute me in the fashion of Spain, hold my stirrup when I mount, and do everything that is required of a servant. Above all, you must not let me oversleep myself, for otherwise I shall be late in arriving at Granada.'

'Sir,' answered the barber, 'I will be as true to you as the dog was to St Dominic. When you are sleeping I will be on guard, and when you are awake I will see that no harm approaches you; but I beg you not to be annoyed with me if, in trying to be of service to you, I do unwillingly cause you any annoyance.'

'Good Pablo,' continued the prince, 'say no more, but return to your shop, pack up your linen, and come here as soon as you can this evening. If I am in bed when you arrive, you will know that it is because I must get up to-morrow morning by five o'clock, and see to it that you let me not sleep beyond that time.'

Pablo hurried home, packed up his few articles of underclothing, and then proceeded to the principal wine tavern to tell his friends of his good fortune. They were all so pleased to hear of Pablo's good luck that they drank to his health, and he returned the compliment so often that at last the wine was beginning to tell on him, so he bid his friends good-bye and left, saying to himself, 'I must wake his highness at five o'clock.' This he kept repeating so often that he had arrived at the large courtyard of the palace before he was aware of it.

The prince's bedroom looked into the courtyard, and Pablo saw by the dim light that was burning in the room that the prince had retired to rest.

Afraid lest the prince should think he had forgotten all about awaking him, and that he might therefore be keeping awake, Pablo seized a long cane, with which he tapped at the window of the prince, and kept on tapping until the prince appeared, and opened the window, shouting out—

'Who is there? Who wants me?'

'It is I,' said Pablo. 'I have not forgotten your orders; to-morrow morning I will wake your highness at five.'

'Very good, Pablo; but let me sleep awhile, or else I shall be tired to-morrow.'

As soon as the prince had disappeared Pablo commenced thinking over all the princes of whom he had heard, and he had become so interested in the subject that when he heard the cock crow, imagining it was daybreak, he again seized the cane and tapped loudly at the window.

The prince again lifted up the sash, and cried out—

'Who is it? What do you want? Let me sleep, or else I shall be tired to-morrow.'

'Sir,' exclaimed the barber, 'the cock has already crowed, and it must be time to rise.'

'You are mistaken,' replied the prince, 'for it is only half an hour ago since you woke me; but I am not annoyed with you.'

Pablo was now sorely troubled in his mind because he thought he might give offence to the prince, and so he kept revolving in his mind all that his mother had told him about the anger of princes, and how much it was to be dreaded. This thought so perplexed him that he resolved on putting an end to the life of the cock that had caused the mistake. He therefore proceeded to the poultry-yard close by, and seeing the offender surrounded by the hens, he made a rush at him, which set all the fowls cackling as if a fox had broken in.

The prince, hearing the noise, hurried to the window, and in a loud voice inquired what the noise was all about.

'Sir,' said Pablo, 'I was but trying to punish the disturber of your rest. I have got hold of him now, and your highness may go to sleep without further care, as I will not forget to waken you.'

'But,' continued the prince, 'if you waken me again before it is time, I will most decidedly punish you.' Saying which he again retired to rest.

'Since the days when cocks crew in the Holy Land they have always brought sorrow into this world,' inwardly ejaculated Pablo. 'His proper place is in the pan, and that is where he should go if I had my way.'

All at once Pablo commenced to feel very sleepy, so he

walked up and down the yard to keep awake; but becoming drowsy he sank on the ground, and was soon so fast asleep that he dreamt a black prince was attacking him, which made him scream so terribly that it woke, not only the prince, but also all the dogs in the neighbourhood.

The prince again rushed to the window, and hearing Pablo scream out, 'Don't murder me, I will give you all!' hurried down into the yard, and seeing how matters stood bestowed such a hearty kick on Pablo that he jumped up.

The frightened barber beholding the prince near to him, took to his heels, and ran home as fast as he could.

When he had got into bed he began regretting that he had run away from the prince's service, so he got up again, saying to himself, 'The prince shall have a sharper spur than I could ever buckle on'; and, proceeding to the principal door of the palace, he wrote the following words with chalk, 'Pablo has gone before your highness to court the Princess of Granada himself.'

This had the desired effect, for when the prince arose in the morning and was leaving the palace alone, he read the words, and they caused him to be so jealous that he performed the distance in half the time he would otherwise have taken.

Pablo after that used to say that 'a jealous man on horseback is first cousin to a flash of lightning and to a true Spaniard.'